AURORA AND THE POPCORN DOLPHIN

Books by Sarah Webb

The Songbird Cafe Girls
1. *Mollie Cinnamon Is Not a Cupcake*
2. *Sunny Days and Moon Cakes*
3. *Aurora and the Popcorn Dolphin*

For older readers:

Ask Amy Green
1. *Boy Trouble*
2. *Summer Secrets*
3. *Bridesmaid Blitz*
4. *Love and Other Drama-Ramas*
5. *Dancing Daze*
6. *Wedding Belles*

AURORA AND THE POPCORN DOLPHIN

Sarah Webb

WALKER
BOOKS

To Alice Mount Stephens,
my loyal reader and friend

First published 2016 by Walker Books Ltd
87 Vauxhall Walk, London SE11 5HJ

2 4 6 8 10 9 7 5 3 1

Text © 2016 Sarah Webb
Cover photographs © 2016 Ericka McConnell
and Susanne Walstrom / Getty Images
Little Bird Island map by Jack Noel

The right of Sarah Webb to be identified as author of this work
has been asserted by her in accordance with the Copyright,
Designs and Patents Act 1988

This book has been typeset in Berkeley

Printed and bound in Great Britain by Clays Ltd, St Ives plc

British Library Cataloguing in Publication Data:
a catalogue record for this book is available from the British Library

ISBN 978-1-4063-4837-8

www.walker.co.uk

Dear Reader,

Thank you for picking up *Aurora and the Popcorn Dolphin*. I've been fascinated by dolphins and whales for a long time. When I was nine I tried to teach myself how to speak humpback whale by listening to a record of their amazing song. Strange but true! The record came free with a copy of *National Geographic* magazine and it was one of my prized possessions. Every day after school I'd shut myself in my room and wail and moan like a humpback. My mum used to rush into my room, thinking I was ill. If you've ever heard a humpback whale singing, you'll know why she thought that.

There are lots of dolphins in the waters around Ireland, which is where I live, and I've been lucky enough to see them on many occasions. I've seen whales, too, in both Ireland and New Zealand.

I had so much fun researching this book, and I learned a lot about sea mammals along the way. I used some of my (and Rory's) favourite dolphin and whale facts to write the quiz at the back of this book. Do try it!

Rory, the main character, has a very special bond with dolphins. I hope you enjoy reading her story.

Best and many wishes,
Sarah XXX

MAINLAND

SEAFIRE
POINT

HORSESHOE
BAY

SUNNY

LOUGH
CARA

BLIND
HARBOUR

CARA
WOODS

SOUTH
HARBOUR

FASTNET
LIGHTHOUSE

REDROCK
VILLAGE

RORY

The
Songbird
Cafe

PRIMARY
SCHOOL

RED MOLL'S
CASTLE

BULL
ISLAND

LITTLE
BULL

MOLLIE

THE ATLANTIC

N
W   E
S

Little
Bird
Island

Chapter 1

Six months ago my life was perfect. I lived in a beautiful white house overlooking the harbour in Stony Brook, Long Island. I had tons of friends. I was captain of the school swim team. I went diving every weekend with my mom, helping with her dolphin research.

But then everything changed.

Today was the last day of summer term. I'm home from school now and I'm sitting in the kitchen with Magda, our housekeeper, watching her cream potato with the hand blender (yes, I'm that bored!) and listening to her humming away to herself, when Dad walks in. "Hey, kiddo," he says. He always calls me that. It was cute when I was little, but now it's kind of embarrassing.

"You're early," I say. Dad's rarely home for dinner. He's a marine biologist, and when he gets caught up in his work, he loses all track of time. He's been working even harder over the last few months and I've barely seen him. "Bad day at the office?"

Dad laughs. "No. Wanted to see my favourite girl."

"Your only girl," I say, then quickly add, "Your only *daughter*", when his face drops and I realize what I've said.

"So what's for dinner, Magda?" he asks a little too brightly, ignoring my correction.

"Steak with peas and cream potato," Magda says, "and vegetable lasagne for Rory. That good, Aidan?"

"Perfect," Dad says, winking at me. "Gotta love your mashed potato, Magda."

Magda serves mashed potato with everything – chicken, steak, pot pie, the works. I love Magda. She started off as my au pair, but now she pretty much runs the house. She's from Slovakia and she's always calling me "darling", but she pronounces it "darlink". She can always make me smile. Not as much as Mom did, though. Mom sure could make me grin.

Mom was hilarious, and I'd laugh so much at her jokes that I practically couldn't breathe and my eyes would well up – like when she used to do crazy robot dancing in the kitchen or when she'd hold out her hand and say, "Shall we dance, Princess Aurora?" and she'd waltz me around the room. That's my real name, Aurora. After I turned six or seven, Mom was the only person in the world I let call me that. To everyone else, I'm just plain old Rory.

Magda goes home after she's served dinner. "See you tomorrow, darlink," she says, giving me a hug. "Bye, Aidan."

I hate it when she goes. Without her, the house always seems too quiet. Dad and I don't chat much these days. We just concentrate on eating. Mom was the talker of the family, and she liked to catch up on all our news while we ate. Dad's reserved and a bit awkward, I guess, like a grown-up geek. I'm never quite sure what's going on his head and lately I don't know what to say to him either. Mom was the glue, sticking us all together. Without her, our tiny family of two just doesn't seem to work.

"How was your last day of middle school, kiddo?" Dad asks as soon as we've finished our food.

"OK," I say, shrugging. The last day of term was pretty uneventful. We had our graduation ceremony a week ago, which was meant to be the main celebration. Dad managed to miss it, though, as he'd gotten the time wrong. He didn't show up until the end of the picnic. That would never have happened if Mom had been around.

Magda was at the ceremony with me. She gave me silver earrings in the shape of dolphins and made a fuss of me, but it wasn't the same. I wish Mom had been there. It didn't feel right without her. I think Dad felt the same way. He just stood under a tree, reading something on his cell the whole time and avoiding everyone.

My friends went shopping with their moms to find cute outfits for the ceremony. Dad offered to take me, but as we've never been shopping together before – he's not that kind of dad – it would have been too weird. When Magda said she'd go with me, I told her I didn't feel like it, and she understood. In the end, she went to the mall on her own and bought me a navy chiffon dress and silver shoes with a small heel. The shoes were too small and pinched my toes. But at least the hot red blisters gave me an excuse to go home early.

"Have you thought about how you'd like to spend the summer, kiddo?" Dad asks.

"Not really," I say.

"Are you sure you don't want to do swim camp this year?"

I nod firmly. "Positive." I love swimming – gliding through the pool like a dolphin, the feel of the silky water against my skin – but Mom was the one who drove me to all the swim meets and cheered me on from the side. I can't face going to camp this year without her around to pick me up after.

Dad looks sad.

"I'll swim again in the fall," I add quickly. "I'm not giving up. I'm just taking a break."

"Okey-dokey. But you can't sit around the house all day watching bad TV shows and eating junk. If you're certain about swim camp then I have a plan. It may involve some dolphin-tracking, and I know how much you like that."

I used to go diving all the time with my mom, to watch and research dolphin behaviour. Mom was a professor at North Shore University, in the School of Marine Sciences, and she knew everything there was to know about dolphin communication. She'd been studying it for years. There's only one other person in the world who knows as much, and that's Professor Aidan Kinsella, aka Dad. Lots of scientists are researching dolphins' whistles and clicks and what they mean, but Mom wanted to take it a step further. She wanted to prove dolphins name things and "talk" to each other, like humans do, so she could show the world how smart they are. Most people thought she was crazy, but not me and Dad. In fact, Dad was helping by inputting her research into a computer called the D-com. They named it the dolphin dictionary. It's an interactive index of whistles, clicks and body language that Mom had observed dolphins making.

"Where?" I ask him. "Florida?" We've been to Florida heaps of times for Mom and Dad's work. There are lots of dolphins there. In Canada too. I'd be really keen to go dolphin-watching this summer. Dad hasn't been doing much work on the dolphin dictionary since Mom died. It would be great if we could collect more data.

"East," he says. "A lot further east."

I think for a second, picturing a map of the world in my head. "Europe?"

Dad smiles. "Not just Europe, kiddo – Ireland. Mattie Finn, your mom's cousin in West Cork, has invited us to stay. She'd like to meet us."

"But the trip to Ireland was Mom's idea!" I say. We'd been planning a big family vacation to Ireland for my thirteenth birthday in August. Mom was so excited. She'd just reconnected with her cousin Mattie, who she hadn't heard from in years, and was really psyched about it. Mom hadn't been to Ireland since her family emigrated to New York City when she was sixteen. She'd always meant to visit, but what with college and work and having me, she'd never gotten around to it. Mom had started telling me all about life in Ireland when she was a kid and about Mattie, her favourite cousin. She said she'd tell me more and show me her old photos before our trip. I wish now I'd asked her to do it right then and there. I wish I'd made the most of every minute we had together. We can't visit Mom's Irish relations without her, it wouldn't be right.

"I know Ireland will be strange without your mom," Dad says, reading my mind. "But Mattie got in touch and said why didn't we come visit anyway? She really wants to meet us. We can leave it a couple of weeks, if you like, to let you get used to the idea. We don't have to go immediately."

"I don't want to go at all without Mom." My voice catches, but I'm determined not to cry. "Let me stay here, please? You go. I'll be fine. Magda can look after me."

Dad goes quiet for a long moment. Finally, he says, "I hear you, kiddo, honest I do. And I wish things could be different, but they're not and we have to get on with life as best we can. The trip will be good for us – a change of scenery and all that. I think your mom would want us to go together."

I swallow the lump in my throat and blink back my tears. He's right. Mom was big into family trips – she would want us to go. "OK," I say. "I guess we're going to Ireland." Then I say, remembering, "You said there are dolphins there. Can we take our dive stuff? And work on Mom's dolphin dictionary?"

Dad looks awkward for a moment and then says, "We'll

see. I have some other research that I might need to get on with first."

"Dad! The dictionary was so important to Mom. We have to keep working on it."

"And we will, I promise, Aurora."

I wince. It's been years since he's called me that and it sounds wrong. Also, talking about Mom and her research has upset me. "I'm tired," I say. "I'm going to bed. I'll see you in the morning."

When I get to my room, I sit on the edge of my bed and take deep breaths, trying to stop the tears that are pricking my eyes. But it's no use – they fall down anyway, hot and fast.

It's been six months, two weeks and three days since Mom slipped on some ice on the sidewalk when she was walking home from the store. She smacked her head on the corner of a step and died of a brain haemorrhage. "A freak accident," the doctor said. "Nothing anyone could have done."

Since her death, I've found it difficult to care about anything or talk to people. It's like there's this sheet of glass between me and the rest of the world. Everything seems harder, even normal things like getting dressed in the morning.

Dad sent me to a counsellor for a few months. We talked about Mom and how sad and angry I felt that she'd been taken away from me. I'm not so angry any more, but I'm still sad – that hasn't changed. I try not to say much about Mom now, especially to people I don't know all that well. Talking about her, remembering how amazing she was, picturing her in my mind – her shining eyes, her wild curls, her lopsided smile – only makes me sadder. It hurts. Because you only get one mom and now mine's gone.

Chapter 2

Two weeks later, Dad is loading our luggage and his research equipment into the back of a taxicab. I'm glad he's bringing so much stuff with him. We'll need it all if we're going to carry on Mom's work. The driver's helping Dad pack the car. We had to turn the last cab away as the trunk wasn't big enough to hold it all. But this car is big, like its driver – a stocky, red-haired man with freckled upper arms so thick they look as though they'll bust out of his short-sleeved shirt at any minute, like the Incredible Hulk.

I start to heave my case into the trunk, but Dad takes it out of my hand. "Easy there, kiddo. I'll do it. You get in the back. Don't forget your seat belt." Since Mom's accident, he's been obsessed with safety.

"What's in all the silver boxes, man?" I hear the cab driver ask as I climb into the back seat. "They're seriously heavy."

"An underwater computer, sound-recording equipment, a hydrophone," Dad says. "Plus some other things. Just your average vacation luggage."

"Yeah, right," the man says. "You some sort of rock star?"

People often ask Dad this, especially when he's not wearing his reading glasses. It's the long, sun-bleached hair and the deep tan from being on the water. He usually says, "No, but I'm friends with one – a world-renowned geology professor called Gregor, who studies meteorites!" It's a terrible science-geek joke, which proves how uncool Dad really is.

This time he just laughs. "Marine biologist," he says.

The man looks unimpressed. "You study fish and stuff in the wild?"

"Sea mammals," Dad says. "Dolphins. But I'm mostly involved in the techie side of things these days."

The man nods. "My kids, they like that dolphin stuff. SeaWorld. Flipper."

I shudder. I hate those places.

"Flipper, sure," Dad says, catching my eye. He hates SeaWorld too, but I guess he's keeping quiet because he doesn't want to start an argument this early in the day.

Wild animals, especially super-smart ones like dolphins and orcas, shouldn't be taken away from their families when they're babies and kept in tanks and made to entertain dumb tourists. It's not right, and it sends them crazy.

Years ago, when she was at college, Mom studied captive dolphins at an aquarium for her marine-science course and realized that they were all making the same low, flat whistle – a sound that wild dolphins don't make unless they are resting or on their own. She figured out this was their "bored" whistle. She also told me about how orcas' dorsal fins curl over in captivity. Orcas are also called killer whales – but they don't kill people, not in the wild, anyway.

Once the trunk is loaded, we pull away from the house.

"So where are you good people off to this fine morning?" the cab driver asks.

"Ireland," Dad says. "Visiting relatives."

The man chuckles. "No kidding! I'm Irish. My grandfather came from County Kerry."

"My great-grandfather was from County Galway," Dad says. And they're off, swapping stories about their family roots.

I stare out the passenger window at the homes and shops we pass on our way out of Stony Brook, trying not to think about Mom and how we're leaving her behind.

Dad and I don't talk much on the flight from New York to Dublin. He tries to get me to chat, but I don't feel like it. I know I should be excited about visiting Ireland, but I'm in a funny mood, flat and low. I don't feel ready to visit Mom's family without her. Honestly, I don't think I'll ever be ready. But it's happening now, whether I like it or not.

It's an overnight flight and I manage to sleep for a couple of hours and doze the rest of the time. We arrive in Dublin airport at eight a.m. local time, stiff and tired. After collecting our baggage – which takes ages because of all Dad's research equipment – we step out of the airport building into the fresh, *cold* air. I had no idea it would be so freezing. My toes are turning into popsicles in my flip-flops. Dad was right to nag me to pack all those fleeces. At least it's not raining. I forgot to pack the rain jacket Magda bought me. It was hard to say goodbye to her. She gave me a big hug, saying, "I will miss you, darlink. Take care of each other, understand? I will see you soon."

"Here we are," Dad says. "Ireland. Pretty, isn't it?"

We're standing in front of a large concrete multi-storey car park.

"OK, maybe not that particular building," he adds quickly.

We pick up our hire car – an old navy Land Rover – and then drive through Dublin. The city is small, and there are no skyscrapers like in American cities, but the old stone buildings and the metal humpback bridge across the river are – yes, I have to admit – pretty. But it's all so grey: the buildings, the shops and even the sky, although there are patches of pale blue behind the clouds. Still, it's supposed to be summer!

We stop off at a store in the city centre to collect extra diving gear, filling the jeep with yellow dive tanks and attaching a large orange RIB – rigid inflatable boat – to our tow hitch. It's the kind of boat with a solid hull and bouncy rubber sides.

Dad hooks his iPhone up to the jeep's stereo and clicks on a Garth Brooks song.

I groan. "Dad!" He doesn't even like country music.

He grins. "What do you want to listen to then?"

I shrug. "Something Irish."

"U2?" he suggests. "They're from Dublin."

"Fine. Or how about something from this century, like Hozier? He's Irish."

"You like Hozier? I didn't know that. Me too."

"There's a lot you don't know about me. I'm full of secrets," I say.

"An international woman of mystery?" he says with a smile. That's from *Austin Powers*. He loves old comedy movies. Action movies, too.

I laugh, and just like that the tension between us starts to melt. "Sorry about yesterday," I say. "I just wasn't in the humour for talking."

"I hear you, kiddo. I get like that myself sometimes. Don't worry about it."

The drive to West Cork, where Mom's relations live, takes for ever. Luckily, I sleep across the rear seat for most of the journey down the highway. Dad insists I wear my seat belt, so it is twisted around me awkwardly.

We stop at a McDonald's along the way, in a place called Cashel. The food tastes just the same as back home, which is kind of weird but reassuring too. We wouldn't have stopped here if Mom was with us. She hated Mickey Ds, as she used to call it. Said the food tastes of cardboard and all the packaging waste isn't good for the planet. She's right, of course, but I'm so hungry today that I eat two veggie wraps with my fries. Like Mom, I'm a vegetarian.

Thirty minutes later we reach the outskirts of Cork city

and find a sign saying "N71 West Cork and Redrock". After a while, the road narrows to one laneway and goes all small and twisty. I start to feel car sick, my head and stomach both spinning, so I lie down across the rear seat and close my eyes again.

When we finally stop, I open my eyes – I must have dozed off again – and sit up. The sky is clear and the sun has finally started shining.

We're parked in front of a tiny harbour, where a small, red car ferry is docked. Behind us is a row of brightly painted shops, cafes and bars. It all looks old-fashioned and quaint, like a picture postcard. There are people sitting outside one of the bars, smiling and chatting. Mom would have gone straight up to them, sat down and started chatting. She must have loved this place. It's so pretty.

"You're awake," Dad says, turning round in his seat.

"Where are we?" I ask, stretching my arms over my head.

"Redrock. Your mom's relatives live over there." He points out to sea.

"In the ocean?" I ask with a smile. "They're mermaids?"

He laughs. "No. On the island, of course."

"I was joking, Pops. Little Bird, right?" I remember the name from Mom's stories.

"Correct. Although there is selkie blood in your mom's family, if you believe in that kind of thing."

"What's a selkie?"

"They were seal people. Half human, half seal. There are

22

old Celtic myths about them. Fairy tales."

I'll bet Mom believed in selkies. She was a scientist, but that didn't mean she ruled out things that science couldn't explain, like the Loch Ness Monster in Scotland or Ogopogo, the Canadian lake monster. Unlike Dad. "If there was something that big in the water, don't you think we would have found it by now?" he was always saying.

"Oh, Aidan." Mum would sigh, her eyes twinkling. "'There are more things in heaven and earth, Horatio, than are dreamt of in your philosophy.'" (It was her favourite quote – Shakespeare, I think.) "They only discovered the giant squid in 1925, remember? And we've only explored five per cent of the ocean. Who knows what else we'll find? I'm keeping an open mind." And so am I.

Dad gestures out to sea again. "The waters around the island are full of marine wildlife, and it's one of the best places in Ireland to study dolphins."

"Perfect for some research then," I say and Dad smiles. Mom told me all about the island's dolphin, Click, and how she used to swim with him. She'd be so psyched to visit Little Bird again. Thinking about her and how much she'd adore being here with us makes me sad. Mom's happy freckled face floats in front of my eyes and I blink to drive it away.

"Is there a pool on the island?" I say, trying to distract myself. "I want to keep fit for the swim team."

Dad gives a laugh. "Rory, it's an island. It's surrounded by water. You can swim every day if you like. With supervision.

In a wetsuit, because the water will be very cold and I don't want you getting hypothermia. And you need to be careful of barnacles when you're getting in and out of the water. They can give you a nasty cut."

I roll my eyes. "Dad! Quit worrying. It's a tiny Irish island. Nothing's going to happen to me. I'll be just fine."

Chapter 3

I stand against the railings of the ferry, the wind whipping my hair, watching the grey and green island get bigger and bigger. Not that it gets much bigger, it's pretty small. There's only a smattering of houses on it, some with metal buildings beside them – farms, maybe.

According to the guidebook I found in the cabin of the ferry, we're in Dolphin Bay and the boat will dock in Dolphin Harbour. I breathe in the air. It's cool and fresh like Canadian air and it catches at the back of your throat. Mom always said the air in West Cork smelled and tasted different – tangy like the sea – and she was right.

As the ferry pulls in alongside the pier, I spot a woman sitting on the harbour wall. She's wearing faded denims with blue paint splattered down one leg and a white shirt tied at her waist. She has a heart-shaped face, with a slightly pointed chin, a button nose and a mop of wild, curly blonde hair.

Mom?

I shield my eyes from the sun and look closer. Of course it's not Mom – but this woman could be her twin. It must be

Mattie, Mom's cousin. I feel that familiar lump in my throat, and I take a deep breath and then blow it out slowly, trying to make the wave of sadness stop. This is the island where Mom spent all her summers, where she first fell in love with dolphins. It's a special place. Of course being here when she's not is going to make me sad. I have to accept that. It doesn't make it any easier, though.

The woman catches the thick rope that one of the ferrymen is throwing at her and loops it over a bollard on the edge of the pier, as if she's been doing it all her life. She probably has.

"Ready?" Dad appears beside me. "That must be Mattie up there," he says. "She said she'd be here to meet the ferry. She sometimes works on the ferry, but she's off today. She's the image of your mom, isn't she?"

I nod.

Mattie spots us then and waves. "Aidan?" she cries, squinting. "Is it Aidan?"

Dad waves back a bit awkwardly. He's shy. The opposite of Mom, who would have hollered over and introduced herself. I can hear her happy, excited voice in my head. "Hey, is that you, Mattie?" she'd say. "We're here – your awful American relatives." She would have leapt off the ferry, dashed up the stone steps and thrown her arms around her cousin, hugging her tight.

"And you must be Rory," Mattie shouts, breaking into my thoughts. "You're very welcome to Little Bird, both of you. Let's get you off the ferry and up to the house. Cal's dying to meet you."

* * *

Driving the heavily laden jeep off the ferry – over a thin metal ramp that looks ancient and rusty – is terrifying. I can tell Dad is anxious too. He's blowing his hair out of his eyes in little puffs and he's gripping the steering wheel so tight his knuckles are white. But it all goes without a hitch, and once we're safely on dry land, Mattie pulls open the front passenger door of the jeep and swings herself in.

"It's so great that you're both here," she says, shutting the door. "Now, let's get you home. I'm dying for a cuppa. We can do all the hugs and kisses when we get there. Do Americans do kisses? Maybe that's just the Italians. French too, yes? Some of them do two kisses, don't they? Now which is which, I wonder? I can never remember." Mattie is clearly a talker, just like Mom.

"I've never been to France or Italy," Dad says. "Only London and Germany and Norway. They're not big into kissing at dolphin conferences."

Mattie gives a hearty laugh. "Good one, Aidan."

I don't think Dad was joking.

"So, which way?" he asks.

"That-a-way." She points at a white stone house on the hill overlooking the water. "It will take us all of two minutes. There aren't too many roads on the island. This is Harbour Road. We live at Harbour Cottage." She chatters on as Dad drives. "How was the flight? OK, I hope. And the drive? I did warn you the road from Cork city to here was kinda twisty, didn't I?"

"You did," Dad says. "And you weren't wrong. But we're here now."

"That you are," she says. "That you are. Safe and sound."

There's a silence then, and I know we're all thinking about Mom, who didn't make it safe and sound.

Mattie starts to tell us about the island and how big it is (tiny – only seven kilometres squared, which she says is about five and a half miles squared) and how many people live here (one hundred and eighty-nine at last count, but that swells in the summer, apparently, with the tourists and the families who stay here during the holidays. She calls them "summer people").

It doesn't take long to get to Harbour Cottage. It's small – just one storey – and it looks ancient. The window surrounds are painted cornflower blue and there's washed-out blue and green sea glass and midnight-blue mussel shells set in an arch around the front door, which is one of those old-fashioned ones you see in books, with a horizontal split halfway down. I've never seen one in real life. There are funny-looking pots, made of green plastic netting, in a pile to the left of the door, and beside them two long red kayaks are tucked against the garden wall.

After I've jumped out of the jeep, Dad parks it. Then he and Mattie unhook the RIB from the back. Like Mom, Mattie seems pretty handy. When they're finished, and Dad has checked and double-checked the RIB's brake and put rocks under the wheels just to be sure, Mattie leads us towards the house.

"Leave your bags in the jeep for the moment," she says. "We can move them later. You must be gagging for a sip of tea. Sorry, the garden is a bit of a mess." She kicks one of the net pots with the toe of her work boot. "Cal was supposed to be mending these lobster pots, but they've been sitting here all week. You know what boys are like." She smiles at me. "Although it's not just boys. Margo was messy too as a teenager. Did she change?"

"No," Dad says, answering for both of us. "Margo never liked cleaning up. Said it was a waste of time. Didn't she, Rory?"

I shrug. I'm still thinking about the empty space in the car where Mom should have been.

"I'm so glad you're here," Mattie says. "I'm just sorry Margo isn't with you. You must miss her desperately."

The truth of this hits me so hard that I don't know what to say. Dad looks close to tears too. People back home aren't usually so direct about Mom.

"Sorry," Mattie says quickly. "My mouth is running away with me again. I didn't mean to upset you, Aidan."

"No, it's all right," Dad says. "We should talk about Margo more. It's just … you know. It's very soon."

Mattie gives him a gentle smile. "I understand."

The door swings open then and a boy comes through it.

"Cal, this is Aidan and Rory," Mattie says.

"Hiya," the boy says easily. He's carrying a pair of board shorts and a towel. He has jet black hair and olive skin and looks nothing like Mattie, apart from his chocolate-brown eyes.

"You're into swimming, aren't you, Rory?" Mattie asks.

"Yes," I say. "That's right." Dad must have told Mattie all about me. Or maybe it was Mom.

"Cal's going swimming with his friends in a while," she says. "Why don't you take Rory with you, Cal? Show her the island?"

"Sure," Cal says, with a weak smile.

He doesn't seem that keen on me tagging along and I feel embarrassed. Dad makes it worse by saying, "I think I should come with you."

"I'll be fine, Dad," I say, cringing. He's treating me like a little kid.

"But you don't know these waters, Rory," Dad says. "We've talked about this, remember? You need to stay safe."

"She'll be fine, Aidan," Mattie says. "Cal's a good swimmer and he'll keep an eye on her, won't you, Cal?"

"I will," Cal says. "I promise, Aidan."

"Then I guess it's OK," Dad says reluctantly. "But make sure she doesn't stay in the water too long, Cal, and if you see any jellyfish—"

"Dad!" I say. He's so embarrassing.

Chapter 4

Harbour Cottage is small but cosy. There's a kitchen to the left of the hallway, with a big pine table, an old black range and a window overlooking the sea. To the right is a small living room; there's also a study and some bedrooms. The floors in the hall and kitchen are tiled with grey slate, and the bedrooms have old wooden floorboards.

"I hope you'll be comfortable in here, Aidan," Mattie says, showing him a bedroom with sunny yellow walls. "It was mine when I was a girl. I've put Rory down the hall. You know, Rory, your mum and I used to sleep in this yellow room during the summer. It had bunk beds in those days. This was my parents' house. They left it to me when they died. Margo used to spend most of July and August here. She loved this island. It's changed a lot since those days, but, look, I found this when I was clearing up." From the wooden dresser, she picks up a faded photo of three girls in a silver frame. The girls' arms are thrown around each other's shoulders, their hair is damp, and they're all wearing plain navy or red swimming costumes.

I recognize Mom immediately. I've seen pictures of her as

a girl before. For some reason, she's the only one not smiling.

"That's you, isn't it?" I ask Mattie, touching the head of the girl with the same curly hair and brown eyes as Mom.

She nods. "Sure is. And the girl with the red hair is Ellen McCarthy. She lived on the island too. She's dead now, bless her. She was Mollie's gran. You'll meet Mollie when you go swimming. She's one of Cal's friends. That photo was taken after our annual swimming race on Horseshoe Strand. I won and Margo wasn't too happy about that, as you can see from her expression. She was pretty competitive. Speaking of swimming, let's go and find Cal."

He's sitting at the kitchen table and jumps up as soon as we walk in the door. "Can we go now, Mum?" he says.

"Where are you headed?" she asks him. "Horseshoe Strand?"

"Yes," he says. "Mollie and Landy are probably there already."

She smiles at him. "Hold your horses. I need to get some tea and a snack into Rory first. She'll need the energy to fight off the cold."

Cal sighs. He's definitely not keen on taking me with him.

"You can go on without me," I tell him. "I don't mind."

"Not at all," Mattie answers for him. "He'll stop being so impatient and he'll wait politely for you to eat, won't you, Cal? Don't roll your eyes at me, young man. And while you're swimming, Rory, I'll help your dad unload the jeep. You can check out the rest of our humble abode later."

* * *

"Dad, stop it, all right," I say when we're waiting for Cal on a wooden bench outside the front door of Mattie and Cal's house. Cal is inside, fetching a towel for me. "Please don't come with me, it would be really embarrassing. I'm twelve, not two. I'll be careful, and Cal said he'd keep an eye on me, remember? We've already been over this."

Dad touches my arm. "I know, but I just want to keep you safe. What's so bad about that?"

I shake off his hand and hug my swimming bag harder against my chest. "I'll be fine. I'll stay within my depth. You've got to stop all this worrying." Dad's always been a bit of a worry wart, but since Mom's accident, he's got so much worse. He won't let me do anything. It's like being back in kindergarten.

"Are you serious, Rory? It's the Atlantic Ocean, not a swimming pool. Jellyfish for a start. And sharks."

"Dad, even I know that sharks don't generally attack people. Aren't you supposed to be the expert?"

"What about hypothermia then? It's not like Stony Brook. The water around here comes from the Arctic. You'll freeze if you stay in it for more than a few minutes. People die from hypothermia. It's no joke."

"It's sunny. Well, sunny-ish." There are a lot more blue bits behind the clouds than there were in Dublin. "I'm not going to die of hypothermia. Are you for real? Please, stop worrying, OK? Just let me go swimming, alone, without my dad watching – like a normal girl."

33

Cal walks out of the house then, a rolled-up blue-and-white striped towel under his arm. He smiles as he hands it to me. "Ready?"

"Thanks, Cal." I shove the towel into my bag and then jump to my feet. I'm dying to get away from Dad. He's starting to seriously bug me.

"It's going to be cold, I warn you," Cal says.

"I did try to tell her—" Dad begins.

"Dad!" I say. "I'm a strong swimmer. You know that. Please?"

"Like I said, I'll keep a good eye on her, Aidan," Cal says.

"You make sure you do that," Dad says firmly. "OK, Rory, you can go on your own. Cal, I'm relying on you."

How humiliating! Cal must think I'm such a child.

"Sorry about that," I say, as we walk away. I can feel Dad staring after me. "Dad can be a little overprotective sometimes."

Cal gives a dry laugh. "Parents, eh? My mum drives me crazy. She never stops talking. Sorry," he adds quickly. "I didn't mean to remind you of … you know… And I'm sorry about the accident and everything. I heard what happened."

"Do you mind if we don't talk about it?" I say, my voice coming out small and strangled.

"Yeah, of course, sorry." He stares down at his feet.

We don't say a word to each other the rest of the way. I can't think of anything to say and he's probably afraid he'll upset me again or offend me or something. I'm such a klutz.

* * *

As soon as I dip my toes in the water on Horseshoe Strand, I squeal. I hate to say it, but Dad was right – it's icy. I pull my foot out quickly. "Is it always this freezing?"

Cal laughs. It's less awkward between us now that we're on the beach with his friends.

"No," he says. "It's usually much colder. It's balmy at the moment." He's already been in the water. He swam the whole length of the bay twice. He's a strong swimmer. I have to admit I'm impressed.

"It's not so bad if you run in quickly," Mollie says. She's small, with friendly blue eyes and the most amazing shock of curly red hair I've ever seen. Like Mattie, she's very chatty. She's wearing green-and-white flowery surf shorts and a turquoise rash vest, not a tiny string bikini like some of the girls back home wear on the beach. Bikinis are no use for swimming in and I'm not into sunbathing. What's the point of sitting around on your butt when you could be in the water?

Landy's nice too. He has messed-up dark blond hair, nutty brown skin and he smiles all the time. My friends back home would love him – but I'm not interested in boys. Not in that way. Not yet. Doesn't stop me noticing them, though, and I can't deny he is cute.

"Come on." Mollie grabs my hand. "We'll run in together."

"No!" I cry, laughing and running away from her. "It's too cold!"

"Rory!" Mollie yells, sprinting after me. "Come back here, you chicken."

I let her drag me towards the breaking surf. When we run into the water side by side, I shriek loudly. The water is freezing!

"I can't," I splutter. "Too cold."

"Don't stop now, you're almost there," Cal shouts from the beach. He's sitting on the sand beside Landy now, beach towels draped over their bare shoulders.

"It's torture," I shout back. "You guys do this for fun?"

Cal laughs. "Go on. I'll buy you both a hot chocolate at Alanna's afterwards."

"What's Alanna's?" I ask Mollie.

"He's talking about the cafe at the harbour. Our friend Alanna runs it. Her hot chocolate is to die for. It's worth a quick dip. On three. One, two, three—" She lunges into the water and starts swimming.

I take a deep breath and force myself to dive in. As soon as my head touches the water, I get brain freeze. I come up after only a few strokes under the surface. My teeth are clenched against the cold. I can only manage to swim a couple more strokes. Usually I power through the sea, but the icy water is making me sluggish and slow. *Stay with it, Rory,* I tell myself. *Keep moving, fast. You'll soon warm up.*

I pull my arms through the water and kick my legs as hard as I can until I start to get into the rhythm: stroke, stroke, breathe, stroke, stroke, breathe. The sea here may be cold, but it's amazingly clean and a beautiful shimmery sapphire blue.

I swim the length of the strand four and a half times until

36

my fingers are so numb I have to stop. Then I wade towards the shore, annoyed that I have to get out. I'm not a quitter. At home I stay in the water until my arm and leg muscles complain.

Cal cheers. "Way to go, Rory! That was awesome. Hot chocolate is on me."

Chapter 5

We're sitting on a leather sofa in front of the window in the Songbird Cafe, drinking our hot chocolate. It's actually pretty tasty. Not too bitter and not too sweet. Alanna, who runs the cafe, was busy in the kitchen when we arrived, so Mollie popped behind the counter and made it herself. She works here when Alanna needs extra help.

The cafe is bright and airy, with shabby-chic blue tables and chairs. It smells of freshly ground coffee, and baking, which reminds me of Magda, who always makes amazing cakes. Mom baked too – her chocolate brownies were delicious – which is funny because she hated cooking proper food. She said it was boring.

Below us is the harbour, and it's quite a view. It's early evening now, but there are still children playing on the small beach. Some boys are cannonballing from the harbour wall and making big white splashes as they hit the water. Seagulls swoop in the air, waiting for a faded red fishing boat that's chugging towards the island. The whole scene looks like something out of a movie.

"So what do you think of the island so far, Rory?" Mollie asks.

"It's pretty. But the water could be warmer." I shrug. "I guess I'm missing home a bit." The truth – that it's Mom I'm missing – is too close to the bone to talk about.

"It took me a while to settle in too," Mollie says with a smile. "I used to live in Dublin, which is much bigger than Little Bird. But I love it here now. You'll get used to the cold sea and the quiet."

"It is quiet, all right. Don't you guys get bored?" I say.

"I thought that too at first," Mollie says with a laugh, but Cal and Landy exchange a glance. They don't look impressed.

I shouldn't have said that – it just slipped out. I didn't mean to be rude about the island. It's their home, after all. I can feel my cheeks get hot.

Since Mom died, I've found conversations, especially ones with people I've just met, difficult. I often seem to say the wrong thing. I wish I could go back to my old happy-go-lucky, chatty self.

I stand up and murmur, "Just need to use the restroom", before walking towards the back of the cafe. I don't even know if I'm going in the right direction. I just need to get away from Mollie and Cal and Landy for a moment and take some deep breaths. A new place and all these new people – it's overwhelming, and I don't want to say anything else wrong. After I use the rest-room, I'll drink my hot chocolate quickly and then tell them I'm jet-lagged and that I need to get back to Cal's house to rest.

Thankfully I seem to be going the right way for the restroom. At least, I think I am. There's a door that says "Mna" on it and another door that reads "Fir". I stand staring at the strange words.

"Mna's the one you want. It means women in Irish." I look round. There's a girl in a sky-blue apron standing beside me. She's small, with dark brown hair hanging in two plaits. Her eyes are emerald green and fixed firmly on mine.

"Maybe it should just say women then," I say. *Oh no, that sounded rude too!*

"Maybe," she says easily. "But some of the islanders speak Irish and the tourists seem to like learning a few words of our native tongue. Especially Americans. I'm Alanna, by the way." There are tiny gold flecks dancing around in her irises and it's hard not to stare at them. "And you're Mattie's relation from Long Island. Rory."

My eyes widen. "How do you know that?"

She smiles. "It's a small island. Everyone knows everything. You'll get used to it. And do come down tomorrow evening, and bring your dad with you. We're having a Fourth of July barbecue."

With all the travelling and the time difference, I'd forgotten it's Fourth of July tomorrow. Mom was big into parties and celebrations, and she loved Independence Day. It's the first one without her and I'm not sure I want to spend it here, with strangers.

"I think we're busy," I say. "But thank you anyway."

Alanna smiles gently. "See how you feel tomorrow. I'd love you both to come. Any time after five o'clock."

I use the restroom, lingering there as long as I can, washing my hands over and over.

When I walk back out, I hear Mollie say, "Maybe it's jet lag. Mum says long flights can wipe you out. She always needs to sleep after she's been away."

"Maybe. I wouldn't mind, but Mum *told* me I had to hang out with her," Cal says. "I think she's—" Cal breaks off because Mollie digs him in the ribs. He looks up to see me standing by their table.

"I'm heading back to the house," I say, trying to sound normal. "I'm tired and Dad will be worried."

Mollie has gone bright red. I can tell she is wondering how much I overheard. What else did they say about me?

"I'll walk with you," Cal says awkwardly.

"That's OK," I say quickly. "I can find it."

"Don't go, Rory," Mollie says. "We want to hear all about America, don't we?"

"Yeah, sure." Landy nods eagerly. "Do you want a muffin? Or something else to eat?" They're clearly all feeling guilty for talking about me.

"Some other time," I say. I'm in such a rush to hurry out the door that I bang my shoulder on the door frame.

Once outside, I let out a sigh of relief and stop for a moment, trying to get my bearings. Then I spot Mattie's house above the harbour and start heading up the road towards it.

"Rory!" shouts a voice behind me. It's Alanna. She must have followed me out. "You left this behind." She hands me my swimming bag. "You all right, pet? I have some cream that will stop that shoulder bruising up, if you'd like it?"

"Thanks, but I need to get back," I say.

"That's a shame. I have it on good authority that Click wants to meet you." She gives me a wink.

"You mean the dolphin?" Mom told me all about Click. He was young when she knew him so he'd be – I do the math in my head – in his thirties now. Dolphins can live until they're at least forty in the wild. Mom loved him. She played with him every day. He's the reason she wanted to be a marine scientist, in fact, so she could find out more about dolphins.

"He's waiting for you," Alanna says. "Over by Whale Rock. Follow me." She leads me down towards the sea and then she points at a large grey rock that's shaped like a whale's back. And then I see him – a grey bottlenose dolphin, his head poking out of the waves just beside the rock.

"I'll leave the pair of you to get acquainted," she says.

"Thanks," I say.

"You're welcome, pet." She smiles and then disappears back inside the cafe.

I walk down to the pier wall and leave my bag beside some fishing nets. There are seaweedy rocks leading out to Whale Rock and I use them as stepping stones. I almost slip several times in my eagerness to get to Click, but my balance is pretty good, so I manage to stay upright and dry. When I reach the rock, Click seems to have disappeared. I stay there for a moment, disappointed, before turning back.

Then I hear a high-pitched whistle. I turn just in time to see Click dive under the water. He pops up again a second later and soars through the air in a perfect arc, like an Olympic gymnast. He's amazing!

When he resurfaces, he's right in front of me. Head tilted, he whistles again. I know all about the different dolphin sounds, because Mom taught me. Some people grow up with a dog, I grew up with dolphins.

Dolphins make noises at a much higher frequency than humans, but Mom said they're so smart they can still work out roughly what we mean when we whistle back, especially if we use body language, like they do. She was using the data in her dolphin dictionary to make links between descriptions, or human "words", and what dolphins were "saying" when they made certain noises or shapes with their bodies.

So I tilt my head like Click did and make a high-pitched welcoming whistle. If Click were a dog, I'd be saying, "Hello, boy. Want to play?"

Click whistles back. Then he drops under the water and comes up again to my right.

I smile. "Are you playing hide-and-seek with me, buddy?"

He whistles again and bobs his head up and down.

I wish I could slip into the water as well. I'd love to swim with him and pretend Mom's beside me, laughing. She was never happier than when she was playing with her beloved dolphins. But I'm too cold right now to get back in the sea again. Besides, I don't want Mollie, Cal and Landy to see me – not after I told them I was going back to Harbour Cottage to rest.

Clicks gives another whistle. After sinking his head under the water, he blows a ribbon of bubbles out of his blowhole and pops back up again to look at me.

I laugh. "You're quite a character, huh? Do you remember my mom? Her name was Margo Finn and she used to take vacations here a long time ago. She swam with you." A lump starts to form in my throat and I swallow it down.

Click moves closer to me like he's really listening.

"I'm going to take that as a yes," I say. "Mom always said dolphins are as smart as people. She wanted you guys to be classified as 'non-human persons', so no one could keep you in captivity. I wish Mom was still here. I really miss her. We used to talk about all kinds of stuff. She was my best friend. Everything's broken now. There's just me and my dad and we're not a proper family. I'm really lonely, Click. I just feel so sad all the time. I miss her so much. No one understands." My eyes fill up with tears and I blink them back.

Click swims towards me, and I reach my hand down and place it on his head. His skin is cool and firm under my fingers. He feels so solid, so real. We stay there for several minutes before I hear Alanna calling over from the harbour wall. "You found him," she says.

As I lift my hand, Click slips under the water again. Within seconds he's vanished.

I scramble back over the rocks to join Alanna.

"Don't worry, he'll be back," she says when I reach her. "He likes you. You've made a new friend. Are you all right, pet?"

I nod wordlessly.

"I understand how you feel, Rory," she says quietly. "I lost my own mum a few years ago. I still miss her every day. If you need someone to talk to—"

"Thank you, but I'm fine." I grab my bag and start to march up the hill, towards Harbour Cottage, biting back my tears. I know Alanna was just trying to be kind, but I don't want to talk about Mom. It hurts too much.

Chapter 6

Dad must have been waiting outside the cottage for me, because he runs down the hill to meet me. He doesn't look happy. "Finally! Where were you, Rory?"

"Swimming with Cal," I say. "And then we went to the cafe for some hot chocolate."

He looks at his watch. "You've been gone hours. And where's Cal?"

"Only two hours. And Cal's still at the cafe. I came back on my own."

Dad's staring at me suspiciously. "Did you guys get on all right?"

"Yeah, we got on fine." Cal may have upset me, but I'm no snitch. "I didn't know you were waiting for me."

"Sorry, maybe I overreacted a little. I was just worried about you. It's my job to keep you safe. If you're going to be late, can you let me know?"

I nod. "OK. Can I take my shower now? I'm all salty." Saying the word salty makes my scalp itch. I hate having salt in my hair. "Is my luggage inside?"

"Yes, it's in your room – last door on the right. You have an en suite and everything. And don't complain about the water pressure. It's not broken. Irish houses don't have power showers. It's actually Mattie's room. She kindly moved out so that you'll have a sea view. Please remember to thank her. I know you're probably tired from travelling, but manners maketh the man, remember?"

Mom used to say that. She was big into manners. "Please" and "thank you" – or "peas" and "ta ta" – were my first words after "da" and "ma". I know that because she wrote it into my baby journal.

Of course I'm going to thank Mattie for giving me her room. Dad clearly doesn't think much of me if he thinks he has to remind me. "Fine," I say.

He tilts his head, just like Click did earlier. "Is that your word for today? Fine?"

What is up with him? He's being really picky and annoying. I guess we're not used to spending so much time together, just the two of us. Back home, I am in my room a lot and Magda's around too, of course. Recently she's been popping in at the weekends to check we're eating properly.

I don't have the energy to call him out on his comment about "fine" being my word of the day, so I just say, "Yes, it is." With that, I walk into the cottage and down the corridor.

I open the door and almost gasp. My room is … beautiful. There are white curtains with blue butterflies on them fluttering around the open French doors, and there's a stunning view of the sea through the doorway. There's even a small paved patio just outside with a wooden bench to sit on. The walls and the bed linen are all a fresh, crisp white. The old-fashioned pine wardrobe and chest of drawers are also both painted white. Even the wooden floorboards are white, with a soft eggshell blue rug beside the bed. It's like something out of a fancy homes magazine, and it's wonderfully calm and serene, like a beach hut. Mom would have loved it. Even though she was the messiest person in the world, flinging her bag and jacket on the floor as soon as she got in the door, she loved the idea of plain, uncluttered rooms and pored over magazines featuring pretty houses. Now that she's gone, our home in Stony Brook is not only too quiet, it's also too tidy.

My bags are sitting on the floor at the end of the bed. I should unpack, but I don't feel like it, so I pull out my wash things and some fresh clothes. I can't wait to rinse the salt out of my hair. Pity I can't wash the whole day out. Scratch that, the last six months.

"So how was swimming, Rory?" Mattie asks after handing me a plate of quiche and salad, with mashed potato on the side. Magda wouldn't be impressed – the potato isn't creamy. It's thick, with craggy white peaks like icebergs, and it's dotted with pools of melted egg-yolk-yellow butter.

"Cold," I say, instantly regretting it, because Dad immediately says, "I did warn you."

Mattie laughs. "Not exactly tropical, I'll grant you, but

you'll get used to it. I love the way your skin tingles after a dip."

"That's probably frostbite," I say. "There's a pool, right? For proper swimming."

"Sadly not," Mattie says. "We'd love an indoor pool for the winter, but the nearest one is on the mainland, in Rossabeg. About twenty miles from Redrock."

Dad gives me a sympathetic smile. "Sorry, kiddo. Guess the sea it is."

My heart sinks. There goes my training. "I'm not sure I can take the cold," I say. "But maybe I'll get used to it."

Dad turns to Mattie. "Rory's on the swim team back home. She's pretty keen. Likes keeping swim fit."

"You could try kayaking," Mattie suggests. "Cal could get you started. It certainly gives your arms and shoulders and tummy muscles a workout, like swimming."

Cal's concentrating on his plate, shovelling in the food as fast as he can. I remember what he said earlier about his mom *making* him hang out with me, and I squirm uncomfortably. "He doesn't have to," I say. "It's OK."

"No, Cal doesn't mind," Mattie says. "Do you? You'll take Rory out kayaking?"

He swallows down his mouthful. "I suppose." He doesn't exactly look thrilled at the prospect.

"That's a plan then," Mattie says, smiling at Dad.

I feel about as small as a ladybug. Cal's only doing it because he has to, like he only took me out swimming earlier because Mattie insisted. This is going to be a long month.

"I'd love to hear more about your work, Aidan," Mattie says. "Margo told me about your dolphin dictionary, and it sounds fascinating. I can't wait to read it. I see dolphins most days on my sea safaris and I think you're right – they definitely have their own special ways of communicating. We're just not smart enough to work out what they're saying yet."

"I wish everyone thought the same, Mattie," Dad says. "Some of the European marine scientists think we're way off the mark, and that there's no evidence dolphins name things the way we do. One Dutch scientist even told Margo she should be researching more worthy things, like ocean pollution or dolphin diseases."

"I bet Margo told him what for," Mattie says.

Dad smiles. "She told him pollution studies were for scientists with no imagination or heart."

"Ouch." Mattie winces. "Good for her. And tell me about your involvement. You're building a database of all the research, is that right?"

"Yes, she'd collect dolphin data from all over the world and I would cross reference it and try to find patterns or algorithms. Then I'd log it into what we called the D-Com, short for Dolphin Communication Computer." Dad and Mattie talk more about his work as we eat and I tune out a little. I don't know all that much about what Dad does. It's the geeky side of things, and even when Mom was around, Dad and I never really talked about it. I'm not that interested in computer stuff. Mom's research – the "on the water" stuff – is way more interesting. Was. Past tense. I keep forgetting.

Cal is checking his cell under the table. I wish I could do the same.

After dinner, I feel a huge wave of exhaustion and I can't stop yawning.

"You must be wrecked, pet," Mattie says. "Long day for you."

I nod and yawn again. I can barely keep my eyes open. "Thanks for dinner. It was delicious." It really was. I don't know what they put in Irish butter, but it made the potato taste so good, despite the lumps.

"Glad you enjoyed it," Mattie says. "Now off you go to bed. You'll be too tired for it tonight, but there's a telly in the living room if you and your dad want to watch something together another night."

"Thanks," I say. Me and Dad haven't watched a movie together for months. We've kind of got out of the habit, and we don't exactly have similar taste. As well as comedies, he likes what Mom called crash-bang movies – all car chases and fights and no proper talking. Mom and I used to love watching shows set in the past, like *Pride and Prejudice* and *Downton Abbey*, and old movies about friendship and love, like *Beaches* and *Sleepless in Seattle*. But the three of us did watch some things together, natural history stuff like *The Blue Planet* and Pixar movies like *Finding Nemo*.

"And thanks for giving me your room," I add, remembering. "It's beautiful. I appreciate it."

She smiles back at me, her eyes twinkling. "You're welcome, Rory. It's very special having you here. It means a lot to me."

"And to us, Mattie," Dad says. "To both of us."

Back in my room, I'm glad to be on my own again. Mattie never stopped talking the whole way through dinner – asking me and Dad questions about school and work. But Dad's naturally quiet, Cal said nothing and I barely said a word either, so maybe she was just trying to fill the gaps. That was a real Mom thing to do too. She hated awkward silences. She was always the life of the party.

The French doors are still open and I can hear seabirds calling and the distant swish-swish of waves breaking against the shore below the cottage. I breathe in the sea air. It makes me feel calmer.

There's a knock at the door, and before I have a chance to answer, Dad walks in.

"You all right, kiddo?" he asks. "You seemed a bit quiet at dinner."

"I'm just tired, Dad." I want to tell him how unsettled and out of sorts I feel, but I don't know how to explain it, and I'm not sure he'd understand.

"I wanted to give you this." He hands me a large black notebook. I know exactly what it is – one of Mom's dolphin journals. There used to be dozens of them in Mom's office at home, thrown in a box under her desk and stacked untidily on the shelves. She'd been keeping them since she was my age. Always the same notebook: black leather with plain white paper.

When Mom died, Dad and Magda sorted through her stuff and gave all her clothes, apart from a few special outfits like her wedding dress, to a thrift store. Dad cleared out her office, but he kept all her papers and notebooks. He put them in the attic for storage.

"The journal's very special," Dad says. "She wrote it on the island, when she was your age. I thought you might like to read it while you're here."

"Wow, thanks, Dad." Swallowing down the lump in my throat, I take it out of his hands and stare down at it, running my fingers over the waxy black cover. I'm a little overcome. It's like holding a piece of her in my hands.

"I'm glad we're on Little Bird, Rory. This place was very special to your mom." He takes a deep breath and blows it out, making his fringe rise a little. He opens his mouth as if to add something, then stops, looks out the French doors and says, "You've got an awesome view of the sea."

"I know and, don't worry, I'll make Mattie a card to show her how much I appreciate it," I say. "And I'll get her some chocolates or something."

Dad smacks his forehead. "Darn it," he says under his breath.

"What?" I ask him.

"I'm an idiot. We should have bought Mattie a gift from Stony Brook. I forgot. Your mom always looked after that kind of thing."

He looks so upset that I say, "It's fine, Dad, we can get her something here at the store."

He nods. "Good idea. Thanks, Rory. And I'm sorry about earlier. I overreacted when you were late back. I'm glad you went swimming with Cal. I just want to keep you safe, that's all."

"I know, Dad. You keep telling me. I get it, honestly." I give a big yawn.

He yawns too. Mom always said yawns were contagious. "Okey-dokey," he says. "Time for us both to get some shut-eye, kiddo. Sleep tight."

"Bugs bite," I say back automatically. It's what I always said to Mom.

"Bugs bite," Dad says softly.

When he's gone, I flop down on the bed and open Mom's notebook on the first page. Her familiar, looping, spidery handwriting stares back at me. She always wrote in pencil. As I run my fingers over the soft imprint the words have made on the paper, my heart gives a little squeeze. I'd been expecting to see notes and sketches about dolphins, but instead there's this:

1 July
My Dolphin Diary by Margo Finn, age 12 1/2
Location: Little Bird, West Cork
Subject: Bottlenose dolphin

<u>Size of subject</u>: Smallish — I think he's male and pretty young. The island fishermen say he's 2 or 3. They know a lot about whales and dolphins as they see them all the time when they're working on their boats.

<u>Subject's identifying marks</u>: White crescent shape on back near blowhole.

<u>General observations</u>: This dolphin lives alone in the waters around the harbour. Most dolphins like swimming in boats' bow waves, but he tends to keep away from boats unless he knows them. Maybe he doesn't like the noise. I think dolphins have pretty good hearing and they have echolocation, which is using sound to help you find or identify objects. Dolphins make a click and then listen to its echo to work out how far away objects are — and their size and shape. They use echolocation to navigate, to hunt fish and to check if there are any predators near by like sharks. It's a bit like the sonar that bats use, apparently, but more complicated. I read about it in the dolphin and whale book Grandad Finn gave me.

The fishermen call him Click because he makes lots of whistles and clicks.

When I sat watching him today, he looked straight at me. I think he was watching me back! I plan to study him every day and see what I can find out about him and then write it down in this notebook. My Dolphin Diary.

See you later,

Margo XXX

14 July

So I've been studying Click every day and he's pretty smart. Mattie said people swim with him sometimes and I asked Grandad if I could too and he said OK as long as I was careful, stayed near the beach and got out of the water if Click made any funny noises or anything. He said wild dolphins can be territorial and if they clack their jaws at you, it's a sign of aggression. He said he'd come and watch just in case.

Today I swam with Click for the first time and it was AMAZING! He seemed to really like playing with me, and even Grandad Finn agreed he was friendly and clever. He's so fast and he tumbles in the water like an acrobat. Luckily I'm a pretty good swimmer so I could kind of keep up with him. We had so much fun!

19 July

I've been swimming with Click all week. I think he's been enjoying it too because he's been making this same whistle at me before I get in the water and also when we are swimming. I'm convinced it means "play". I've decided to write down all the different whistles and noises and movements he makes and put the meanings beside them. It'll be my very own Dictionary of Dolphin Noises. You never know, maybe one day I'll be a famous marine biologist and publish a book about it!

OK, so meaning number one coming up...

<u>Play:</u> When Click wants to play, he jumps out of the water, plays hide-and-seek with me and makes one long continuous whistle which rises towards the end.

Stay tuned for more meanings once I've figured them out...

Mom was so smart and so dedicated to studying dolphins, even at my age. She was truly one of a kind! And I love the idea that Click inspired her dolphin dictionary. Reading her journal reminds me how excited and passionate she always was, and how much fun we had together. I miss her so much. My tears drop down onto the journal, making the ink blur. I dab the paper dry carefully with my sleeve, shut the book and then curl up on the bed.

Chapter 7

"Happy Fourth of July, kiddo," Dad says, looking up from his dive computer, when I come outside the next day. He's standing beside the Land Rover surrounded by tanks and diving kit. His thick black wetsuit is draped over the roof bars of the jeep, looking like a seal skin. The smaller wetsuit is hanging beside it. They're both extra thick – 12mm – and are made especially for cold water. Dad always checks the equipment carefully before we dive for the first time in a new place.

"What would you like to do this afternoon?" he asks.

I shrug. "I'm not sure. Guess you're going diving?"

"Just getting organized for a dive tomorrow, in fact." Trust Dad. We've only been here one day and he's already itching to get back to work. Mom was just as bad, maybe worse. She would have had us out on the water yesterday. "I'm collecting data on bottlenose echolocation for one of my colleagues. It shouldn't be too hard to find research subjects. Mattie says there are several pods in these waters at the moment and a resident lone male."

"So you're not working on Mom's dolphin dictionary?"

Dad goes quiet for a moment. He stares back down at his dive computer. "Not right now."

"Why not?" I ask.

Publishing the dolphin dictionary as soon as possible is vital. Mom wanted to share her findings with the whole world, because she believed that if everyone knew how amazing and intelligent dolphins are, they might think harder about protecting their natural environment – the sea. She also thought it would help to ban the kind of fishing nets that kill sea mammals. Dolphins were her life. I know that for a fact and Dad does too.

"I just need some time, OK? In fact, your mom and I were kind of on to a breakthrough just before..." He trails off. I see the pain and sadness behind his eyes. He misses Mom so much, I know that. But I can't seem to find the words to talk to him about it, to tell him how much I miss her too.

"Anyway," he says, "we'd been playing with the D-com" – the computer Dad had built to record all Mom's findings – "to see if we could use it underwater to mimic the dolphins' whistles. It's been slow going, but I think we were getting somewhere."

I stare at him in stunned silence. "Are you serious? You mean we'd be able to use it to talk back to dolphins when we're underwater?"

He nods. "In a very limited way, using very limited vocabulary. It may take years to figure out how, but, yes, I think we can do it. Your mom thought so too."

"Why didn't you tell me this before, Dad?" I ask. "Why the big secret?"

He shrugs. "It's at such an early stage. We didn't want to disappoint you. Like I said, the progress has been pretty slow to date."

"I can't believe you didn't tell me. You can't give up on this, Dad."

"And I won't, but I need to get this echolocation stuff done. And I just need a break. A bit of distance from the D-com, to think about things. Can you understand that?"

"I guess."

He gives me a gentle smile. "Thanks, Rory. Until then, this echolocation project is keeping me busy. In fact, I was hoping you'd come out with me tomorrow, be my dive buddy. Just like old times, hey, kiddo?"

Not like old times at all. Mom was my dive buddy, not Dad. Yes, sometimes the three of us dived together, but it's never been just me and Dad, ever. But I can see how much he wants me to go so I say, "OK. I'll dive with you."

"Great. And what are you doing now? How about we go for a tour in the jeep and see a bit of the island? It's small, so it won't take us long."

"Sure." Then I think of something and add, "I don't suppose you'd let me drive a bit or give me a lesson? Mom started teaching me in the fall, but we had to stop because of the ice. And then, well, you know…"

Dad looks shocked. "Really? I know Margo wanted you to

learn to drive young, like she did, but she never said anything to me about giving you lessons." My great-grandfather taught Mom and Mattie to drive in a field behind their house when they were thirteen.

I smile. "Because she knew you wouldn't be keen on the idea, Captain Careful." It's what Mom used to call him when he was being over-cautious.

"Hey, less of the Captain Careful, thank you very much." He sucks his teeth and shakes his head. "I'm sorry, Rory. I don't think it's such a good idea. We'll talk about it again when you're a bit older, OK?"

"Fine," I say. I'm disappointed, but I'm not exactly surprised.

"Ready to tour the island?" he asks.

"Sure. If this thing can make it! How old is it?" I kick the wheel of the jeep with the toe of my Converse. Our jeep back home isn't exactly new, but it's not rusty like this one.

Dad laughs. "Ancient. But her engine has been remodelled."

"Her?"

"Cars and boats are always female. 'Cos they're trouble, like all you girls."

"Hey!" It's such an un-Dad thing to say that it makes me laugh. He's usually so serious. Mom was the joker in our family.

He grins. "Only kidding. Give me a second to clear up and then we'll get going. Can you run inside and tell Mattie that we're going out for a while?"

I find Mattie sitting at the kitchen table, reading something on her laptop. She looks up and smiles at me. "Hi, Rory. I'm just checking the bookings for today. Did your dad tell you about my sea-safari business?"

"A little. What kind of boat do you use?"

"It's a motor boat with a small cabin."

"Do you go out every day?"

"Depends on the weather and if I have enough people interested. It's mainly a summer job; not many tourists around in the winter. I work on the ferry too. You're most welcome to join me on a sea safari any time you like, but I'd bet you've seen more marine life than I could ever show you."

"Thanks." I'm not sure I'd enjoy going out on the sea safari, but I don't want to be rude. Mom had mixed feelings about what she called "tourist boats". Me too. They're good at teaching people about wildlife, but they also pollute the environment. "Anyway, I came in to say that Dad and I are going for a drive. We won't be long."

"Great. I'm working this afternoon, so I'll meet you down at the cafe at five – if I don't see you before."

"The cafe?"

"Alanna's having a Fourth of July barbecue. I promised her we'd be there. Your dad thinks it's a great idea. Cal and his friends will be there too, so it won't be just us oldies. You don't look all that enthusiastic, Rory."

I shrug. "I'm not sure I want to go." I don't feel like telling her that: a, her son and his friends don't like me and, b, I don't fancy celebrating Fourth of July without Mom.

Two deep creases appear above Mattie's nose. Mom used to get the exact same double frown when she was annoyed with me.

"I'm sorry," I say. "I didn't mean to be rude, Mattie. It's just—" I take a deep breath. "I don't feel much like celebrating anything right now." It's the best I can do to explain.

Her expression softens. "I understand. But give the barbecue a try. It might be fun."

Fun? Is she serious? A fake, Irish Fourth of July party without Mom?

"Alanna's a good cook," she adds. "And your dad's promised to help her with the grilling."

"OK, I'll think about it."

"That's the spirit." She moves towards me – I think she wants to give me a hug – but I back away. I'm not ready for hugs from Mattie, not yet. It would remind me too much of hugging Mom.

"Dad's waiting for me," I say quickly. "See you later."

Outside, Dad's busy packing the diving masks and swim fins into a silver case ready for his diving trip tomorrow. He lifts the last of the equipment boxes into the trunk, slams it shut and then gets into the driver's seat. I climb in beside him and buckle up.

"Ready to go?" he asks.

"All set," I tell him. "Oh, and Mattie said she'd see us at the barbecue."

"Everything all right, kiddo?" Dad asks. "You seem a bit …
I don't know, tense."

"I'm OK. Can we go now, please?" I stare straight ahead,
but I can feel his eyes on me.

"Rory, what's wrong?"

"Nothing."

"There's clearly something up. We're not going anywhere
until you've talked to me."

I sigh. "I don't really want to go to this barbecue tonight."

"It'll be fun."

"That's what Mattie said, but it won't. Not without Mom."

Dad goes quiet for a moment. Then he says, "Rory, I
know losing Mom was incredibly hard, but we have to move
forwards, try to get on with our lives, start going to parties
again. Especially ones that have been organized in our honour."

"Really? Alanna's going to all that trouble for us?"

He nods solemnly and I feel bad. It's such a kind thing to
do. "We have to go then, don't we?"

"We sure do. Now let's get going."

As we drive down the road, he starts talking about the
fields and how green they are. I'm only half listening. I'm
thinking about Mom and our driving lessons. Mom started
to teach me last October in a big out-of-town parking lot. But
then winter came in and we had to stop because it got too icy.
I guess we both thought we had all the time in the world. We
were wrong.

Suddenly something darts across the road. It's a rabbit. We

have to stop or we'll crush it!

In a rush of adrenaline, I reach over, grab the steering wheel and turn it, hard. We careen into the hedge at the side of the road.

Dad swears and yanks up the handbrake. We come to a lurching stop. The jeep is buried up to the windshield in a green and pink bush. "Jeeze, Rory! What are you doing?" He turns off the engine. "Have you gone crazy?"

My heart is hammering in my chest and I feel sick. "There was a rabbit. Did it get away?"

"What rabbit?" he asks. "I didn't see any rabbit. It must have run off. We were lucky it was a hedge we hit and not a wall. Let's hope there isn't too much damage to the jeep or to the hedge."

I feel a bit cold and shivery. I think it's shock. "I'm sorry," I tell him. "I was just trying to save the rabbit."

"It's OK, Rory," Dad says. "I'll back out of here and we'll keep going."

"I need to check the rabbit got away," I say and open the door. I wish Mom was here. She would have congratulated me for saving the rabbit's life. She wouldn't have worried about the darn hedge or the jeep's paintwork. "I'm sorry I made you hit the hedge."

After getting out of the jeep, I take a quick look up and down the road and under the car. No sign of a squashed rabbit, thank goodness.

"We didn't hit him," I tell Dad, through his side window.

"Good," he says. "Are you getting back in, Rory?"

I shake my head. I've gone off the idea of a drive with Dad. I need some space right now. "I think I'm going to take a walk instead if that's OK. I'll meet you at the cafe for the barbecue. Five, yes?"

"That's right." He tries for a smile, but it doesn't reach his eyes. "Why don't I drop the jeep back and come with you?" he asks. "You might get lost."

"It's a tiny island, Dad. I'm not going to get lost. I won't go far, I promise. See you." I walk away, feeling Dad's eyes boring into my back.

Chapter 8

After leaving Dad, I walk down the lane towards the harbour. Maybe Click is in the water. I keeping thinking about Mom today and I'm not in the mood to talk to anyone. The only person I want to see right now is Click and he's not even human. How sad is that? Then I remember catching Mom talking to dolphins, not just once but heaps of times. She used to chatter away to them. She said they didn't know what she was saying, but she was sure they understood tone and body language. She was convinced they could tell if she was in a good mood or a bad one. And if she was feeling down, swimming with them always cheered her up. I wish I'd brought my dive suit with me or even my swim suit and then I could slide into the water and swim with Click.

When I reach the harbour, I sit down on the wall. It's quiet down here, and cold. The sun has gone behind the clouds. Everyone must be at home, keeping warm, I guess. I scan the water for several minutes, looking for the sleek grey curve of Click's back, but it's no use – he's nowhere to be seen.

I look up when I hear someone walking towards me. It's

Alanna. "Looking for Click?" she says. "Stand on Whale Rock and whistle for him. It always works for me. I can show you, if you like?"

"Thanks," I say.

She hands me a rolled-up towel. "There are swimming togs in there in case you want to go for a dip. They're brand new, a present for you. Wild dolphins don't always take kindly to humans in their water – they see it as their space, as I'm sure you know – but Click's different. He's a gentle soul."

"My mom used to swim with him when she was a teenager," I say, surprising myself. I hadn't meant to tell Alanna that. I don't normally talk about Mom with strangers. "She went on to be a marine biologist. She researched bottlenose dolphins like Click."

Alanna smiles. "She must have been a very smart woman. And no wonder you're so good with Click. You must have learned a lot about dolphins from her work. Drop into the cafe after your swim, if you like. You might need a hot chocolate to warm you up. And I'll keep an eye out the window in case you need a hand getting out of the water or anything. The rocks can be slippy."

Alanna's offer makes me feel safe. I don't know these waters – there might be currents or something. Also, the idea of someone watching out for me when I'm swimming alone would make Dad happy. I nod gratefully and give her the best smile I can manage. She's so kind. A lump forms in my throat and I swallow it down. "Thanks," I whisper.

"You're welcome, pet. Enjoy the water. I'll go and call Click for you." With that, she jumps down off the pier and makes her way carefully towards Whale Rock. Once there, she cups her hands around her mouth and whistles loudly.

Within seconds Click appears in the water, and then his head pops up just beside Alanna. She turns round and grins at me. I give her a wave.

When Alanna's back inside the café, I find a secluded spot and change into the emerald green swimsuit. After leaving my clothes wrapped up in the towel, I walk across the pier, the stone smooth under my feet, and lower myself off the edge. Then I walk to Whale Rock just like Alanna did.

"Wait for me, Click," I call over to him and he looks at me, opening and closing his mouth a couple of times. Then he ducks his head under the surface, squirts water out his blowhole and pops back up.

I recognize the gesture immediately. "You want to play, do you, buddy?" I smile and give a long continuous whistle that rises at the end. Mom taught it to me years ago. It means "play".

Click tilts his head and gives the same whistle back. Then he bobs his head under water.

"That's right, play, buddy," I say. "You understood me, didn't you? Clever Click. Let's play then."

I lower myself into the water, squealing as the iciness pricks my skin.

"I'll be with you in a second," I say. "I need some of your blubber to protect me from the cold. OK, here I come."

I kick away from the rocks and dive under. Then I open my eyes. They sting at first, and it takes a few seconds for them to adjust, which is why I feel Click beside me before I see him. When my vision clears, I get a fright and gasp, taking in a mouthful of salty water, because he's right in front of me. His beak – or rostrum (Mom taught me that word when I was three!) – almost touches my nose. Choking, I swim to the surface to breathe. I've been this close to hundreds of dolphins, but usually I'm fully suited up, with a mask over my face, an oxygen tank strapped on my back and swim fins on my feet. Right now I feel exposed.

Click surfaces with me. He makes a long chirping noise as I cough and splutter, almost as if he's saying sorry for frightening me. Then he flicks water at me with his flipper. I hear Mom's voice in my ear saying, "Pectoral fin, Rory, not flipper", and it makes me smile.

"Let's try that again, buddy," I tell him after I've recovered. "How about playing the seaweed game with me?" I grab a long rope of slimy brown seaweed from the rock. "Mom used to call this stuff Deadman's Bootlaces," I tell Click with a grin. "Nice name, huh?" I loop the seaweed over my right arm and dive under the water.

Click follows me and I swim hard, pulling my arms through the water and letting the seaweed float behind me like a dark ribbon. Then I stop, remove the seaweed from my arm and hold it out towards Click. He takes it from me and balances it on his beak.

I nod and then swim away from him. He follows me and then tilts forward so that the seaweed drops off his beak towards me. It's the dolphin version of "Fetch" and it's something Mom and I did a lot with dolphins on our research trips. It's a great way to explore how they interact with each other and with us – plus, it's fun.

My lungs are starting to sting, so I surface again and gulp in air. Once I have my breath back, I say, "Good boy, Click. You're one smart dolphin." I give him a wide, toothy grin. He opens his mouth wide too. It's almost like he's grinning back at me.

I laugh. "You sure are something, Click. I can see why Mom loved you."

When I get back to Harbour Cottage after playing with Click and popping into the cafe to say thank you to Alanna (and drinking one of her delicious hot chocolates), I sneak into my room through the French doors so Dad doesn't catch me and ask why my hair's wet. He wouldn't be thrilled about the idea of me swimming alone. I strip off my clothes and stand in the shower, letting the warm water wash the salt off my skin. It takes several minutes to stop shivering. I stayed in the sea far too long – until my fingers were numb and my teeth were chattering – but it was worth it.

After my shower, I get dressed and sit on the bed, pulling my brush through my wet hair. Drops of water fall onto the white bed linen, making damp splotches. I grab a towel and twist it into a turban on my head, like Mom used to do. Then I spot Mom's dolphin journal on my bedside table. I open it up, dying to read more about Click.

7 August

Today I was watching Click from Whale Rock when he did something really strange. He was swimming just outside the harbour when a small pod — 3 female bottlenoses and 2 babies, the same species as Click — appeared. He kept his distance from them until a small fishing boat approached the harbour and then he went crazy. He jumped out of the water and curved his body into an S shape. I've never seen him do that before. Then he whistled loudly — four short ones that he repeated over and over. It was like he was trying to catch the other dolphins' attention.

Sure enough, they seemed to listen to him. They moved away from the fishing boat, anyway, and swam back out into the bay.

Afterwards, I asked one of the fishermen if he had seen Click do the S shape before or give that double whistle. He said Click always did this around boats if there were other dolphins in the water. He reckoned Click was letting other dolphins know that boats could be dangerous because Click got that crescent mark on his back when he got too close to a fishing boat. Its propeller cut into his skin.

So I now have a second listing for my Dolphin Dictionary:

72

<u>Danger:</u> When Click senses or sees a dangerous situation, he repeats two short whistles over and over.

This has been witnessed by me, Margo Finn, but also by a Little Bird fisherman.

Sometimes the whistle is accompanied by an S-shaped body posture.

"Rory!" I hear Dad's voice outside the bedroom door. "Can I come in?"

I look at the clock beside my bed. Oops, it's almost five and my hair's still wet from the shower. "I'll be out in a minute. I'm just getting ready."

"We're going to be late for the barbecue," he says. "Mattie and Cal have already left."

"I said I'd meet you there, Dad. I'm not quite ready yet," I say.

There's a long pause. "Okey-dokey." His voice sounds a bit flat. He's probably worried about going to the barbecue on his own. Dad is really shy. Mom was the loud, outgoing one.

"I'll walk down with you," I say. "Give me ten minutes."

Lame Irish barbecue, here we come.

Chapter 9

When Dad and I arrive at the cafe, Alanna is just inside the door. I think she was waiting for us. "Howdy, American friends and honoured guests," she says. "Ready for our rootin' tootin' Fourth of July barbecue?" She's wearing a brown cowboy hat and a T-shirt with George Washington on the front that says "May the Fourth be with you".

"Great T-shirt," I say, meaning it.

She grins at me. "Thanks. Amazing what you can find on the Internet. We're all in the backyard." She's still talking in a terrible American accent. It's so bad it makes me smile.

"Are you supposed to be from Texas?" I ask her.

"Correct, little missy," she says, then turns to Dad. "And is my grill chef all primed and ready?"

"At your service, ma'am." He salutes playfully.

I stare at him in surprise. He's not usually a fun, jokey kind of guy.

There are about twenty people in the yard behind the cafe. They're all sitting around wooden picnic tables that are covered in jaunty red gingham tablecloths. There's cute American-flag bunting strung over them, and a large old-fashioned charcoal grill is smoking away in the far corner, sending wafts of spicy, meaty cooking smells into the air. I wrinkle my nose.

"There are plenty of veggie burgers and salads too if you're not a carnivore," Alanna says, reading my mind. "And lots of cakes, if you have a sweet tooth like me."

She's not kidding about there being a lot of food. The trestle tables along the back wall of the cafe are covered in plates of burgers, chicken wings, potato salad, coleslaw and corn on the cob, as well as cupcakes with stars-and-stripes icing, red-white-and-blue fruit platters (strawberries, baby marshmallows and blueberries) and chocolate brownies decorated with tiny American flags on cocktail sticks. The sight of the brownies reminds me of the ones Mom used to make. They were amazing – all moist and chewy and not too sweet. I take a deep breath. *Try not to think about her,* I tell myself.

I take back everything I said about this barbecue. I thought it would be terrible, but it's not – it's awesome.

"You've gone to a lot of trouble, Alanna," Dad says, echoing what I'm thinking.

"I love parties," Alanna says. "Any excuse. And here you go, MasterChef." She takes a sky-blue Songbird Cafe apron and a tall white chef's hat from one of the trestle tables and hands them to him.

He puts them on, and I laugh. "You look like a real pro, Dad." Then I remember that we haven't had a barbecue since

Mom died and the smile drops off my face.

"You going to be OK while I help Alanna and Mattie grill, kiddo?" he asks me.

"Cal's over there with Landy and the girls," Alanna says, pointing at a table. "You should go and join them."

My stomach clenches nervously. Will they want me to sit with them? But Dad's looking at me so hopefully and I don't want to let him down. I know how much he wants me to join in and "have fun".

"OK," I say. "See you later, alligator eater." It was something Mom used to say.

"In a while, crocodile," he says back.

Our eyes meet and I know Mom's on his mind too.

I walk slowly towards the picnic table where Cal and the others are sitting, wondering what reaction I'll get.

"Rory, over here!" Mollie says, shuffling down the bench to make room for me. She's wearing an "I Love New York" T-shirt. "This is Sunny." She introduces the dark-haired girl next to her. "Sunny lives on the island too. Sit down with us."

"Hi, Rory," Sunny says with a shy smile. Her voice is quiet, and I have to strain my ears to hear her. I think she's Chinese, like my friend Wei back home. She looks at me for a moment, then blinks a few times, glances down at the table and adds, "I've heard lots about you from Mollie."

They're being so friendly that I start to feel better. Then Cal looks at me and I go all awkward again. He's sitting with Landy and they're both wearing cowboy hats – small black ones with white fringing, like you'd get in a toy store.

"Sorry about yesterday," Landy says. "We didn't mean to make you feel unwelcome."

"Especially on your first day," Cal adds. "What you overhead yesterday in the cafe... We'd like you to hang out with us, honestly."

Mollie nods. "We really would."

I think about this for a second. I have two choices here. I can tell them all to go take a hike or I can swallow my pride and accept their apology. And even though I'm still a bit annoyed with them for talking about me behind my back, I pick option number two – let it go. "Be the bigger person," Mom used to say.

So I shrug and say, "Sure. I was a bit jet-lagged yesterday, like you said, Mollie."

"How are you feeling today?" she asks kindly.

"Better," I say. "Ready to hang out with my cousin, even if his mom is forcing him to be nice to me." I turn towards Cal, who looks sheepish.

"Ouch, I deserved that," he says. There's a slightly awkward silence for a second, then he asks, "So this whole Fourth of July shindig is in your honour then?"

I shrug again. "I guess."

"Way to go, Rory," he says with a grin. "I can't wait to get stuck into the food."

Mollie rolls her eyes. "Boys. Always thinking of their stomachs."

Sunny and I smile at her.

"So you're from New York, right?" Sunny asks in her soft voice.

"Long Island," I say. "New York State. A town called Stony Brook."

"And you're staying with Cal?"

I nod. She meets my gaze for a moment, and it's clear Mollie's told her all about Mom. I start to tense, waiting for her to say, "I'm sorry about your mom", or something like that, but she just gives me another shy smile and stares down at the table again. "It's nice to have you here, Rory," she says and leaves it at that.

I take an extra deep breath, relieved.

"We're going kayaking down the rapids tomorrow, Rory," Mollie says. "Would you like to come with us?"

Cal adds, "You should definitely come. We can take the big kayaks. There's a seal colony there."

"Are you sure you want me tagging along?" I ask him.

"Yes. Honestly. But don't mention the rapids to your dad or my mum. If anyone asks, we're paddling on a nice, calm lake called Lough Cara. Mum's already said that's OK, if we're careful and stick together."

I smile. "Got it. I'd love to, thanks."

"Come and get your burgers and hot dogs," Alanna says loudly. "Beautifully cooked by Mattie and our genuine American chef. A big round of applause for Mr Aidan Kinsella, please."

Everyone claps and cheers, especially Cal and Landy. "Get along there, little doggie, this buckaroo here needs a feedin' from the chuck wagon," Landy says, sounding completely crazy.

Mollie laughs so much she spits Coke all over the table. It even comes out of her nose!

"Yuck, Mollie, gross," Landy says, but she just laughs again.

"It's your fault," she says. "You sound insane."

"You don't like my cowboy accent, purdy lady? Shame on you."

After the food, Alanna forces us all, even Dad, to line-dance.

"Are you ready, cowboys and cow gals?" she says in her fake Texas accent after we've cleared away the tables. "Achy Breaky Heart" is playing on the stereo. "Here we go."

I feel really stupid, but I don't want to be the only one not joining in. I need to show everyone I can be outgoing and fun, even if I don't feel it inside.

"First we're going to learn a few steps," Alanna says. "The heel dig. Dig your heel into the ground like this." She demonstrates and we all copy her. "Awesome, everyone," she says. "Now the vine. Step right, cross your left foot behind the right foot…" We follow her instructions again and several people, including Landy, fall over their own feet.

"Let's try that one again, line-dancers," Alanna says. "This time try not to trip, Landy."

We soon get the hang of it, and ten minutes later we're all

line-dancing to "Cotton Eye Joe". I never thought I'd see Dad do heel digs and jazz boxes, but here he is, dancing away.

"You're really good at this, Rory," Mollie says at the end of the song.

"We did some line-dancing at school," I say – which isn't true, but I don't want to tell her that Mom taught me. She'd looked it up on the Internet. Mom was like that – she always wanted to find out how to do new things. She would have loved this barbecue: the decorations, the food, the dancing. My eyes start to blur with tears, and I excuse myself to fetch a glass of water. Then I stand by the wall, sipping my drink and watching everyone else. I feel even sadder when the next song comes on. It's "Galway Girl", which was one of Mom's favourites, because of the Irish connection. Dad doesn't seem to have noticed what song is playing. He's hooked his arm through Mattie's and is twirling her around. His cheeks are bright red and he has a wide happy smile on his face.

It hurts to see him. How can he be having fun like that when Mom's not here?

"You OK, Rory?" I look round to find that Mollie is standing beside me.

"Mom loved this song." The words are out of my mouth before I can stop them. I instantly regret it. "I'm a bit tired," I add quickly. "I'm going to go back to Cal's house. Can you tell my dad for me?"

"Sure. Would you like me to walk with you?"

"No, I'm good. But thanks for offering. And it was nice to

meet your friend, Sunny. Can I ask you something? Is she very shy? She didn't really look at me when she was talking."

"It's pretty amazing she can chat to you at all," Mollie says. "She only started talking to me last month. She had an anxiety disorder and she could only speak to her parents and her sister before that."

"Wow. I feel bad for saying anything. I'm sorry. She seems really cool."

"She is, and it's all right – she wouldn't mind me telling you. It's better that you know. She does go quiet sometimes. Anyway, you'll see her again tomorrow when we go kayaking."

I nod, although I'd forgotten. I'm still miles away, back in the kitchen at Stony Brook with Mom. "Yes. See you then."

I walk up the hill towards Mattie and Cal's house with the last verse of "Galway Girl" ringing out from the cafe. The singer is talking about waking up alone, with a broken heart, as his love had abandoned him.

Broken heart? I feel my own heart squeeze. That song could be about me.

Chapter 10

"Did you have fun at the barbecue last night?" Dad asks me the following morning at breakfast. Mattie is already out – she's taking a group of wedding guests on a private sea safari – and Cal's still in bed, so it's just Dad and me. He made pancakes, which is another thing he hasn't done since Mom, well, you know. They were pretty tasty, even with honey instead of maple syrup.

I shrug. "It was all right."

"Are you ready for our boat trip today?"

I stare at him blankly for a second or two and then I remember. I promised yesterday that we'd go out diving together. "Cal asked me kayaking with him and some of his friends. Can I go with them instead? Do you mind?"

Dad doesn't answer for a moment and I can tell he's not keen on the idea. "Are there are any adults going?"

"We're just paddling around a small lake on the island – we'll be fine. Cal says it's really calm. I'll wear a buoyancy aid."

"OK," he says. "I suppose it's good for you to spend time with Cal and other kids your own age. My research trip can wait until tomorrow. But just be careful on the water. You can roll your eyes at me all you like, but drowning is the third leading cause of accidental death."

"You've told me that before, Captain Careful. And I'm always careful around water, you know that."

He frowns. "Less of the Captain Careful, thanks, and promise me you won't do anything stupid."

Four hours later, Dad's words – "Don't do anything stupid, Rory" – come back to haunt me. I'm standing on a platform over Lough Cara, wearing the wetsuit I borrowed from Mattie (my diving wetsuit is too thick for kayaking) and staring down at the swirling black water with white tips below. Mollie and Sunny are next to me. They're also watching the fast-running rapids, as are Cal and Landy.

I thought Cal was joking when he said "rapids" but clearly not. The lake is wide but narrows below us before going out to sea, so the rapids are caused by water flooding in and out of that channel.

The lake is beautiful. It's surrounded by old mossy trees, and the water is insanely clear. Mom must have loved it. We even saw a seal earlier – he popped up and swam a few yards with us, before diving back under the water.

Landy's dad kindly dropped us, along with the three kayaks, off at the lake in his jeep. He didn't know we were headed for the rapids, though, so he left us on the other side. We had to paddle over here. Sunny took the single kayak, and Mollie and

I took one of the double ones. The boys took the other.

Mollie and I raced the boys here, and almost won. My arms are strong from swimming, which helped, and Mollie's competitive, like me, so she took the race very seriously. "Let's get those suckers," she yelled. "Put your back into it, Rory. Let's go, Billy-o."

"Hey, Rory," Mollie says now. "The first rule of Rapid Club is that there is no Rapid Club, got it?"

I stare at her, confused. "What?"

Landy grins. "Mollie's a movie geek, pay no attention to her. That's from *Fight Club*. Which she hasn't actually seen as it's for over-eighteens."

Mollie sticks her tongue out at him. "I can still quote it."

"And she's right," Cal adds. "Rory, you can't tell your dad or Mattie we were up here. Especially Mattie. Got it?"

"Why?" I ask.

Landy and Cal exchange a look.

"Because the grown-ups think it's a wee bit dangerous," Landy says.

"Is it?" I ask.

"Not if you stay upright," he says. "You've been kayaking before, right?"

I nod. A couple of times, on the beach, where the water was really calm and flat, but I don't tell him that.

"Maybe this isn't such a good idea," Cal says.

Landy thumps him on the arm. "Chicken. She'll be grand."

"Who are you calling chicken?" Cal play-punches him back and Landy almost falls over the ledge and into the water.

"Guys, be careful," Sunny says. She turns towards me. "Are you sure you want to do this, Rory?" she asks gently. "You don't have to."

"Is it fun?" I ask her.

She nods and smiles. "Amazing fun."

Mollie grins too. "Brilliant fun."

"And you've both done it before?" I say.

"Lots of times," Mollie says. "In a kayak and on a body board."

I shrug. "In that case, let's go for it."

We make our way back to the kayaks, which we left pulled up onto the rocks at the start of the rapids.

"Let's all go together in the big kayak," Mollie says to Sunny and me.

"Great idea," Sunny says. I'm relieved and instantly feel less nervous.

The two of them hold the kayak steady as I step into it. It wobbles a bit as I wiggle my butt into the seat, press my feet against the footrests and grip the black paddle with both hands. Sunny climbs in behind me and then Mollie in front of me, and once they are both settled, Mollie says, "Let's follow the boys." Landy and Cal are already paddling towards the swirling water in the other double kayak.

"What do we do when we're actually in the rapids?" I ask.

"Nothing," Mollie says. "Just sit back and enjoy the ride."

"Here we go!" Landy yells as he and Cal start to speed down the swirling currents, hooting and cheering as they go. Seconds later, our kayak is also sucked towards the deluge.

And then we start to move faster and faster until the kayak whooshes down the wild froth, the front of the boat dipping under the water and then bobbing up again, like a dolphin's beak. Water slams over me, and I squeal, shaking my head to get it out of my eyes. It's icy cold, but because I'm hot after all the paddling, I don't mind.

"Wow!" I shout. "This is awesome!"

"Told you it was fun," Mollie yells back at me.

Seconds later, the rapids spit us out at the other end of the channel and our kayak drifts along for a few yards before slowing down and finally stopping. Landy and Cal paddle towards us. They're both soaked too. Landy's blond hair is now dark from the water and slicked back off his face.

"So, what do you think, Rory?" he says.

I smile at him. "Can we go again?"

He grins. "Sure. But first we have to get these babies back up the rapids. Hope you're fit."

"If you can't manage it, we can lift them out and carry them back along the platform," Cal says.

"We'll manage it, won't we, girls?" I say firmly.

Mollie turns around and pulls a face. "We can try. It's pretty difficult."

"You'll be grand," Landy says. "Keep in to the sides and paddle as hard as you can."

Mollie's right – getting up the rapids is no joke. You have to paddle twice as fast just to stay in one place. The first time we try it we get halfway up before we are swept back down to the end again, which is very frustrating. But I'm determined that if Landy and Cal can do it, we can too.

On the third attempt, we make it. I'm exhausted, though, and Mollie and Sunny are also puffing and panting.

Cal is waiting for us at the start of the rapids. He's in the one-man kayak this time. There's no sign of Landy.

"Hey, Cal," Mollie calls over. "Where's Landy?"

Cal points to the water with his paddle, and I see that Landy is bobbing in the water beside the kayak. "He's swimming down. Or floating more like."

"With no kayak? Is that safe?" I ask Mollie.

She nods. "Yes." Then she adds with a slight frown, "As long as he doesn't hit his head on a rock."

It doesn't sound very reassuring.

"Don't worry," Sunny says. "His buoyancy aid will keep him upright. He'll be fine."

Cal has paddled out so that his kayak is pulled into the fast-running water. It's smaller than ours and it shoots down the rapids like a bullet. Landy is just behind him, whooping as the water smacks him in the face and sends him swirling around like a spider in a plug hole.

Sunny sits this one out, saying she needs a rest, so Mollie and I follow the boys in the double kayak. I don't enjoy the ride so much this time because I'm worried about Landy smacking his head on a boulder.

"You OK, Rory?" Mollie asks after we've shot out the end of the rapids, soaked again. "You're very quiet."

"Sure," I say. "Just taking in the scenery." I give her a smile.

In front of us, Cal is paddling towards a group of dark grey rocks on the right-hand shoreline and Landy is swimming along beside him. Suddenly one of the rocks starts to move. It's not a rock at all – it's a seal! It glides down the seaweed, into the water.

"Seals!" Mollie says. "Let's go and see." We start paddling towards them.

I can now see that there are lots of adult seals on the rock. They are all watching us warily. There are four or five baby seals with them, which are small and really cute. From their size, I'd say they're only a few weeks old. Another of the adults splashes quickly into the water, followed by the babies and a third adult. They disappear beneath the surface. Then several other adult seals slide off the seaweed and begin to swim towards Cal and Landy until they're surrounding them. I've never seen seals act like this. The seal nearest Landy starts to make a low barking noise, like a guard dog.

"There's something wrong with them," Mollie says. "They're usually really friendly."

A seal's head appears beside our kayak. It's smaller than the others – a female, I guess. Mom used to love seals. She said they were the dogs of the sea: loyal and kind. And suddenly I realize why the seals are acting like this. They're protecting their young. They think we're a threat. We don't mean any harm, but they don't know that.

"They're worried about their babies," I yell at Landy. "Swim away from the rocks, slowly. They'll let you pass."

"Are you sure?" Landy says. "They're freaking me out."

"Swim towards the rapids, Landy," I say firmly. "You'll be fine. Trust me, OK?"

"He's not going to hurt your babies, I promise," I tell the mother seal beside our boat. I know she can't understand me, but I hope that something in my tone or in my eyes will make her see that we don't mean any harm.

"Do what Rory says," Cal tells Landy. "I think she's right. They're starting to move away already."

Landy swims slightly frantically back towards the platform at the end of the rapids and Cal follows closely behind him in the kayak. The seals are peeling off to the left and right of Landy, letting him pass. Finally Landy pulls himself out of the water and collapses, his body bent over, gulping in air. I think he was seriously scared.

Cal climbs out of his kayak, pulls it up onto the platform and then goes over to check Landy is all right. Mollie and I paddle over to the platform too, and Sunny has run down to join us. Our double kayak is heavy, but with the Cal and Sunny's help, we manage to heave it onto the stony surface. We all sit down to catch our breath.

"Is everyone OK?" Sunny whispers.

"Yes," Mollie says. "Thanks to Rory."

"I'm never going near seals again," Landy says, shaking his head. "Seriously loopy animals. I thought they were going to bite me or something."

"They were just protecting their babies," I say. "They're actually really smart, and loyal, too."

"They're probably scared of humans because of the culling," Cal says.

I stare at him, shocked. "What do you mean?"

"The fishermen around here used to kill seal cubs," he explains. "I don't think they do it any more, but maybe the older seals remember."

"What?" I say. "Why would fishermen do that?"

Landy shrugs. "Because seals eat all their fish."

"That's outrageous!" I say. "They're not *their* fish. And I can't believe you agree with it."

"I don't agree with it," Landy says. "But now I can see why seals annoy people, that's all. They were being pretty aggressive out there. What if they bit a kid or something? They probably have rabies."

I glare at him, my blood boiling. "Those seals do not have rabies. And they never attack humans unless they're threatened. What kind of people are you? Do you agree with killing dolphins and whales, too?"

"Of course not," Mollie says quickly. "But there is a dolphin in Kerry who keeps attacking swimmers."

"I read about that," Landy adds. "He's really dangerous. I think they're putting him down."

"It's his *home*," I say. "The sea belongs to dolphins and seals, not to us! I bet he's attacking humans because he wants them out of his territory. Why don't people just swim somewhere else? Irish people clearly have no respect for sea mammals."

"Hey, that's unfair," Cal says. "We all love them just as much as you do, especially Mum. She's mad about whales and dolphins."

"Really?' I say. "You think driving tourists around in a motor boat helps the environment? If she really cared so much, she wouldn't be polluting the sea with engine oil and she'd leave the animals be." As soon as the words are out of my mouth, I wish I could take them back. Mattie's been nothing but kind to me.

Cal's eyes spark. "Look, Miss New York Princess, it's her job, OK? That and driving the ferry. She works hard; there's not much employment on the island. Why are you being like this? One minute you're acting all friendly and cool and the next you're telling me that Mum's sea safari is rubbish. Make up your mind. Do you want to hang out with us or not?"

"Good question," I say. "If you have such Neanderthal attitudes to wildlife and conservation, I'm genuinely not sure. How can you not realize how much this stuff matters? The world is so fragile and we're destroying it!" I grab a paddle and march over to the one-man kayak and start pushing it into the water.

"Where are you going?" Cal shouts after me.

"It's OK, Rory," Sunny says. "We can carry the kayak back up. You don't have to paddle it."

I ignore her, which isn't very nice, I know, but I'm just too angry and frustrated to talk to any of them. When the kayak is in the water, I climb in.

"You may not get up those rapids on your own, Rory," Cal says.

"Just as well I'm not going up the rapids then, isn't it?" I say and paddle in the opposite direction, away from the seal colony, towards the open water.

"Rory!" Mollie shouts after me. "You can't go that way – it's the Atlantic. The waves are big out there. Cal's sorry for calling you a princess, aren't you, Cal? And I'm sorry too. And Landy is. We're all sorry. We know you care about the environment and stuff. Come back!"

It's too late. I'm overreacting, but I'm too embarrassed and furious with myself to stick around. I just want to get away from them all. I paddle furiously towards the open sea. It's Ireland, for heaven's sake, not Hawaii – how big can the waves be?

Chapter 11

The answer is Irish waves can be huge. I almost turn back, but I can't bear the thought of losing face in front of them all, especially Cal.

I'll show them. I'll get back to Dolphin Harbour, no problem. Little Bird is a tiny island – it won't take me long at all. I concentrate on powering through the lumpy water, putting my whole body into each stroke. I lean forward, dig the edge of the paddle deep into the waves and then pull back, hard, bracing my legs against the footrest and forcing the kayak smoothly through the sea.

The cliffs rise up on my left, menacing and dark. The waves crashing against them are a bit intimidating, but as long as I keep well away, I'm sure I'll be fine. I'm nice and toasty in Mattie's wetsuit, although there is a sharp wind whipping against my cheeks now and I can feel it even through the neoprene. *Pretend you're at a swim race and you're determined to win,* I tell myself. *Focus on every stroke.*

I paddle on for what seems like hours, keeping my distance from the cliffs. The sky is heavy with grey clouds, and the waves are huge. They lift me up and then smash me down again, which makes the going difficult. My arms are tired and my shoulders are stiff. I stop for a moment and roll my shoulders back, but the wind tears into me and I start to shiver. I need to keep moving.

I take some deep breaths and then start paddling again. Within a few minutes my muscles are stinging from the strain of trying to pull the kayak through the waves. But I have to keep going. I'm a long way from the rapids now and there's no turning back. I may not reach Dolphin Harbour, but I'll keep following the coast until I can find a beach. Once I get ashore, I can leave the kayak and walk back to Mattie's house if I have to.

There's a small island ahead of me to the right, with an even smaller one beyond it, further out to sea, and opposite the islands is the headland at the end of Little Bird. I recognize it from the tall white lighthouse standing proudly at its tip. I love lighthouses and I spotted this one from the ferry on Friday. Friday – only two days ago, but it feels like a lifetime. Right now, I wish we'd never set foot on that darned ferry. I should be back in Stony Brook, enjoying the sun, not stuck in this kayak in the freezing Atlantic Ocean.

Concentrate, Rory, I tell myself. *Don't stop paddling.* If I can just make it to the lighthouse, I'll be OK. I may even reach Dolphin Harbour after all.

The gap between the small island and the cliffs is narrow, and the gap between the islands is also narrow, so I decide I'd better go around the outside of both the islands, just in case, even if that means going into open water. I don't want to end up dashed against a cliff-face.

The sky gets even darker and then it starts to rain, the large drops bouncing off the deck of the kayak like a drum roll. Paddling is agony now. I count out my strokes, willing myself to keep going. "One, two, three, four…"

As soon as I reach the far side of the smaller island, I realize I've made a mistake. I should have stuck closer to the land. The waves are even bigger out here and the wind is howling in my ears. I'm wet through and my teeth are chattering.

What was I thinking? The sea is dangerous and you never go out alone – Dad's drilled that into me since I was tiny, and even Mom, the most fearless person in the world, would never go ocean kayaking solo. I know I had to get away from Cal and the others, but did I have to be so dramatic about it? If I hadn't gotten so angry, I could have told them how important seals are to the marine ecosystem. That's what Mom would have done. She would have told them that if we don't do something about the pollution of our seas and oceans, between 25 and 50 per cent of dolphin species will be extinct by 2100. But, no, I chose to run away.

Maybe Cal will tell Mattie where I am, maybe not. I wouldn't blame him if he didn't, not after what I said about his mom's sea-safari business. And if he had told someone, surely they'd be here by now? No, I'm on my own, and I've no one to blame but myself. What happens if I don't make it around this island?

My arms are in so much pain. If I stop, though, the waves

will smash the kayak against the rocks. But I don't know how long I can keep going.

I'm about to lose all hope when I spot something in the water. A familiar dark, curved shape.

A dolphin!

It jumps out of the sea, just ahead of me. Could it be Click? It's certainly the same size. The dolphin swims under the waves and pops up just beside me. It's definitely Click – I can see his white-crescent marking clearly now.

"Hi, Click," I say, my voice broken and shivery. "I'm not doing so good and I sure am glad to see you."

He tilts his head as if he understands, and then he starts to swim beside my kayak, keeping me company.

His presence gives me the strength to go on. Painful stroke after painful stroke, Click never leaves my side. I finally pass the small island and then start to head back towards the headland of Little Bird.

"Nearly there," I tell myself out loud. "Keep going, Rory. You have to keep going." Click's eyes are gentle and kind. He whistles at me and then dives back under the water.

"Don't go, Click!" I shout over the wind, but it's no use – he's swimming away from me. And it's worse than before he was here. I'm exhausted. My arms are so painful I can't take one more stroke. I have to rest. I put the paddle across the middle of the kayak and massage my biceps. As I do, a wave crashes over me and then another and another, soaking my already cold and wet body.

Every wave sweeps me further out to sea. I have to start paddling again, I just have to. And then another huge breaker hits the kayak, and before I know what's happened, it's whipped away the paddle.

"No!" I watch in horror as the waves drag the paddle further and further away. I think about jumping out and swimming after it, but that would be stupid. "Stay with the boat," Mom and Dad taught me when I was little. "Whatever happens, always stay with the boat."

"Mom, if you're up there, looking out for me," I cry, "please bring Click back. I'm scared and I don't want to be on my own. Please, Mom, I'm begging you."

Another huge wave crashes over me, and I'm so scared that for a second I don't hear the splash of something surfacing beside the boat. Then there's a whistle, and when I look down, I see that Click is back. I've never been so pleased to see anyone in my whole life. "Thanks, Mom," I whisper. Then I hear another noise behind me, a faint chugging, like an engine. I turn to look. There's an orange RIB powering through the waves towards me.

I feel a surge of adrenaline and relief. Someone's come to look for me. I'm safe. I start waving frantically. "Over here!" I shout as loud as I can. My voice is shaky and weak, but I keep shouting and thumping the sides of the kayak with my freezing cold hands. "Here!"

As the boat draws closer, I spot Dad at the wheel in his yellow oilskins, with Mattie just behind him.

"Rory!" Dad hollers over the noise of the wind, as he pulls alongside the kayak. "Thank God you're safe." The kayak is smashing against the padded side of the RIB, but Dad and Mattie manage to pull me into their boat. Then Dad wraps me in a silver emergency blanket while Mattie secures the kayak to the back of the RIB with its painter.

"What the hell were you thinking, Rory?" Dad shouts. I've never seen him so angry. "I can't believe you took off on your own. You know the rules. After everything that's happened, Rory, how could you?"

I start to cry. I hate myself for putting Dad through this. He's been terrified of accidents ever since Mom died. He was with her, you see, when it happened. I was at the pool and they were walking back from the store together. He was carrying a bag of groceries, so he wasn't holding her hand. Mom slipped and banged her head on the icy sidewalk. She died before the ambulance could arrive. A stupid, lousy, senseless accident that wrecked both our lives for ever. Simple as that.

Mattie puts her hand on his arm. "We need to get her back to the house, Aidan. She could go into shock."

"OK," Dad says, his eyes still stormy. "I'll drive. Make sure she's all right, Mattie. I can't look at her at the moment."

Mattie strokes the side of my cold, wet face as the tears pour from my eyes. "Your dad was worried sick, Rory. Don't mind him. He's just upset. He was afraid he'd lost you."

I give a small nod to show I understand. "I shouldn't have gone off on my own," I say. My teeth are chattering and I can barely get the words out. "It was stupid. Tell Cal I'm sorry."

"You can tell him yourself soon," she says. "The others, too. They're all back at the cottage, waiting for news. They sent us out to rescue you, but we were starting to give up hope. We were looking for you on the wrong side of Bull Island. Luckily, we followed Click, or we might not have found you in time. He's special, that dolphin. Margo was right."

My eyes fill with tears again. All I can do is nod. Looks like I have my very own dolphin guardian angel.

Chapter 12

As soon as we get back to Harbour Cottage, Mattie runs a warm bath for me and peels me out of the wetsuit. My hands are shaking so much I can't even undo the zip.

Dad is the kitchen talking to Cal, Mollie, Landy and Sunny. I could hear their murmured voices as I staggered past the closed kitchen door. I was glad Dad and Mattie didn't make me go in and talk to them.

"You gave your dad a right scare," Mattie says, testing the temperature of the water with her hand while I stand there shivering in my swimsuit. "Cal too. He told me about the seals and your argument."

"I'm sorry," I stammer, wondering if he also told her what I said about her work. I can feel my cheeks burning at the thought of it.

She smiles and strokes my hair. "It's OK, Rory, I'm not mad. Boats do pollute the sea, but I hope the sea safari does some good, too, by showing visitors to the island our wildlife. I do talk to them about ecology and protecting our animals' natural habitats."

I feel terrible. "I shouldn't have said that. I was just … I don't know…" I break off. I want to explain how I sometimes feel annoyed and frustrated and fed up with the world. Having to live without Mom is horrible. And, if I'm honest, I feel angry with Mom most of all, for leaving me alone like this. It's hard to admit – I mean, hating my mom for dying, I must be some kind of monster, right? There's no way I can say that out loud, not to Mattie, not to anyone.

"It won't always be this hard, Rory, I promise. Give yourself time." And I know she's talking about Mom. "Now, have a good soak, and afterwards I'll make you some hot chocolate and a sandwich – you must be hungry. I'll send Cal and the gang down to Alanna's, so you and your dad can have some privacy. I'm sure he'll want to talk to you about what happened."

My stomach lurches. I'm in for a long lecture. But what I did was stupid and he has every right to be furious with me. I must have really scared him.

"Don't worry about it too much," Mattie says, reading my thoughts on my face. "He's only angry because he was worried about you. It was Cal's fault really for taking you to the rapids in the first place. I had no idea he would be so irresponsible. You're only twelve and Mollie's not much older."

"I'm nearly thirteen! And please don't blame Cal for me running off on my own like that."

Mattie sighs. "I guess there's no point going over and over it now. You're back safe and sound, that's what matters. But Cal can kiss goodbye to the rest of his summer. He's going to be working with me every day from now on."

"Please don't do that. He'll hate me."

"No, he won't, he's not like that. And he has to learn to take responsibility for his actions. He lied to me and he put you and the others in real danger taking you to those rapids." Mattie tests the bath water again and, satisfied, turns off the taps. "But don't you worry about it. You're cousins and that means you're allowed to fight. It's the rule. You should have heard the humdingers me and Margo used to have when we were kids. We tore strips off each other."

I look at her, surprised. Mom never said anything about them fighting. "Seriously? What did you fight about?"

"When we were little, toys, and who was better at running and swimming – that kind of thing. Margo was very competitive and she brought out the worst in me. And when we were older, I hate to admit it, but we fought about boys. There were only two lads on the island around our age, and neither of them had any interest in us. Didn't stop us trying to get their attention, of course."

I smile. "Who won?"

Mattie grins. "Your mum, of course, every time. Apart from the swimming races. I was always better than her at swimming, and it drove her crazy. I'll tell you more about it another day. Now, hop into the bath before it gets cold. Call me if you need anything."

She's walking out the door when I call her back. "Mattie? I'm sorry you didn't get to meet up with Mom again."

She nods, her eyes sad. "Me too, pet, me too. She was a wonderful person."

When she's gone, I bolt the door, peel off my swimsuit and lower myself into the bath. The hot water makes my skin sting at first and my butt feel prickly, but I quickly get used to it. I lie back and let the heat soak into my aching shoulder muscles and arms, slowly bringing my whole body back to life.

I close my eyes and think about Mom. She was super-competitive, all right. She'd argue with you, hard, until you backed down, so most of the time it was easier to give up and let her win. She and Dad had big fights sometimes, over silly things. She'd storm out of the house after a row and wouldn't come back for hours. The next morning she'd be back to her old, smiling self, kissing Dad on the top of his head like she always did, as if nothing had happened.

One day I asked her where she went when she stomped out of the house.

"I just go for a stroll," she said. "I walk out my bad mood. I'm sorry, Aurora, I know our arguments upset you. But they're part of life, I'm afraid. Everyone has fights now and then."

"But you still love Daddy, right?" I asked her. "You're not getting a divorce?" My friend Wei's parents are divorced and she only gets to see her dad at the weekends.

"Oh, sweetie, of course I do," Mom said, stroking my hair. "With all my heart."

Mom.

I picture her the last time we were all on vacation together

– in Florida just before the holidays – pulling on her wetsuit before diving, her eyes bright and excited. She'd been teasing Dad, who was having trouble zipping up his wetsuit over his slightly round tummy.

There's a knock on the door, and I jump a little, sloshing water over the side of the bath.

"Rory, everything all right?" It's Dad. "You're very quiet in there. Mattie says your hot chocolate is nearly ready."

"I'll be out in a minute." As soon as I hear him walk away, I sink back under the water. I'm in no rush to talk to him, no rush at all.

"So when does the lecture start?" Dad and I are sitting at the kitchen table. I've eaten a sandwich and now I'm sipping my hot chocolate. It's delicious – the folks on this island sure know how to make hot chocolate.

"Rory," he says, a sharp edge to his voice. "Don't make light of this. What you did was incredibly stupid. The sea's a dangerous place. You never go out alone in any boat, especially a small kayak. I've told you that so many times."

"I know, but—"

"There are no buts. How could you go off on your own? It was reckless, insane. After Mom's accident and everything, how could you take a risk like that? I was terrified something bad had happened to you."

I shrivel a little inside. "I'm sorry, Dad. I should never have put you through that. I wasn't thinking straight."

"Clearly. And you certainly weren't listening to me. Anyway, I've made a decision. No more hanging out with Cal and the others. Tomorrow you're coming out on the water with me, where I can keep an eye on you. And you'll come out with me every day after that until I feel I can trust you again."

"I'm not a kid. I can look after myself."

"You've made it very clear today that you can't. It's my mistake. I should never have let you go kayaking unsupervised. But I trusted you. And you let me down." Dad rubs his hand over his face, and his eyes go all intense again. "I keep thinking about what might have happened if we hadn't found you."

"I would have made it back to Dolphin Harbour, safe and sound."

"Without a paddle?"

"Click would have towed me."

Dad gives a dry laugh. "Get a grip, Rory. You're not living in a storybook. You would have died of hypothermia or been smashed against the cliffs."

I stare at him, shocked. It's not like Dad to be so graphic, so brutal. I must really have worried him. "But it didn't happen, you found me," I say. "I'm fine." Then I don't know if it's tiredness, or stress, or panic about what might have happened, but I suddenly lose my temper. "I'm sorry I'm such a mess. I'm sorry I'm such a bad daughter. I'm just sorry, OK?"

"You're not a bad daughter, Rory," Dad says. "Or a mess. You just do incredibly stupid things sometimes and there have to be consequences. I won't let you endanger your life."

"What life?" I say. "Right now, I don't have a life. Not one I want, anyway. Not without Mom."

Dad's eyes soften. "Don't say things like that, Rory, please. I know you're finding things hard, but it will get easier."

"People keep saying that, but it's not true. Every day I wake up and it's just one more day without Mom."

Dad seems lost for words. He opens his mouth to say something, then closes it again.

"I have to go down to the cafe and apologize to Cal and the others," I say, filling the long silence. "Mattie says they're all down there. Not that they'll want to see me. I've probably ruined their summer. But I want to get it over with. And you're not coming with me. That would be way too embarrassing."

Dad nods. "It's a good idea to say sorry, Rory. How long are you going to be?" He looks at his dive watch.

"Are you timing me?"

"Yes. It's almost seven. If you're not back by seven thirty, I'm coming down to find you, friends or no friends. You need to go to bed and rest. We've both had a difficult day."

"Fine. I won't be long." I don't bother correcting his use of the word "friends". There's no way they'll want anything to do with me, not now.

"And I really am sorry," I add.

Dad sighs deeply. "I know, kiddo. I know."

Chapter 13

As soon as I walk in the door of the cafe, I instantly regret my apology plan. Cal, Mollie, Sunny and Landy are all sitting together in front of the window. Cal looks angry. He's saying something to the rest of the gang and I'm sure it's about me. Then Mollie spots me and looks a little panicked. She talks to Cal, who turns round and gives me a dark scowl. "You're not welcome here," he says.

Mollie gasps. "Cal!"

"What?" he says. "She's wrecked my whole summer."

"It's not her fault," Sunny says.

Cal isn't budging. "Yes, it is. If she hadn't taken that kayak and nearly got herself killed, I wouldn't have to spend the rest of my summer working with Mum. For free – she's not even paying me."

"I'm sorry," I murmur, really embarrassed. He's being so loud everyone in the cafe has turned round to see what's going on.

He snorts. "Yeah, right. And saying all that stuff about Mum's work, unbelievable. She was so excited about meeting you and your dad. Talk about ungrateful. And you've got the others in trouble too."

"Really?" I ask, horrified.

"Yeah," Landy says glumly. "I haven't told my parents yet, but I'll probably be grounded when they find out."

"They've probably already found out," Mollie says. "Nothing stays secret on Little Bird. Nan's going to kill me. And your parents will be mad too, won't they, Sunny?"

Sunny gives a little shrug and I know she's trying not to make me feel worse.

"Happy now, Rory?" Cal asks. "You've ruined everyone's summer. Come on, guys, let's go. I don't want to hang around if she's here." He jumps to his feet and walks towards the door.

Mollie gives me a shrug and says, "Sorry, Rory. He's a bit upset. We'd better keep him company. I'm sure he'll calm down soon."

I nod. "That's OK. See you. And I really am sorry."

Sunny gives me a gentle smile. "Take care, Rory," she whispers before following the others out of the door.

I'm left there standing on my own, feeling like a complete loser.

"What can I get you?" someone asks. It's Alanna.

"Nothing," I say. "I'm just going."

"You sure?" Her eyes are warm and kind. "I could use some help closing up. I can pay you in chocolate brownies."

I'm in no rush to get back to Mattie's house, where I'm everyone's least-favourite person, and I have half an hour until

Dad enacts his one-man search party, so I shrug. "All right," I say. "What do I have to do?"

After telling the remaining customers that she's about to close, Alanna shows me how to clear the tables, wipe them down and lift the chairs off the floor so we can sweep up. After that, we stretch Saran Wrap (she calls it "clingfilm") over the bowls of salad and put them in the fridge. She cleans all the kitchen counters with bleach while I box up the biscuits and cakes.

"Don't forget to put aside some of those brownies for yourself," she reminds me.

"You're a good worker," she says when we've finished. We flop down on the sofa in front of the window, where Cal and his friends had been sitting. "You must have been a real help to your mum," she adds.

I give a laugh. "Mom was so messy. She hated cleaning and vacuuming. Said it gave her hives. We have a housekeeper, Magda. She cooks, too. We're pretty lucky. She's kind of like part of the family." I wonder what Magda's up to back home. I miss her funny expressions and her strong hugs. I could do with one of her bone-crunching hugs right now.

Alanna smiles. "You sure are lucky. I'm not a big fan of cleaning either. But when you run a cafe, it has to be done. My mum always said that a tidy house was the sign of a wasted life."

"My mom would have agreed with that! What happened to your mom?" I ask. "You said she died."

Alanna stares out of the window, her eyes focusing on the water. After a moment, she says in a low voice, "She was driving to Limerick with Dad to collect me from my auntie's house. It was icy and a truck skidded into them. They were both killed instantly."

I wince. Poor Alanna. "That's awful," I say. "Who looked after you?"

She's still gazing out of the window. "I lived with my aunt and uncle for a while. But I missed the island, so I moved here and stayed with my nan." She looks at me. "This is her place, in fact. Nan left it to me when she passed away. There's an apartment above us."

"You live here on your own?"

"Yes. But I'm never lonely. There's always someone popping in to say hi. And my aunt and uncle and my cousins come every year for Christmas and New Year's Eve. It's a family tradition. Mum was big into family traditions and festivals. She'd celebrate anything."

"Even American holidays like Fourth of July?"

She smiles. "Yes. Any excuse for a get-together or a party."

"Sounds like my mom," I tell her. "She loved Fourth of July. And Thanksgiving. And St Patrick's Day, of course, being Irish. St Patrick's Day is big in New York."

"Tell me more about her," Alanna says. "What was she like?"

Mom's face appears in front of my eyes. She's laughing, her head thrown back, her eyes crinkling at the corners. "She looked a lot like Mattie," I say. "Curly blonde hair and dark brown eyes. She was funny. She used to make me laugh all the time. She liked telling me stories about the island and what she and Mattie used to get up to. And about Click. She played with him when she was a girl. She loved him so much."

Alanna looks amazed. "The same Click? Can dolphins really live that long?"

"Yes, they can live up to forty in the wild."

"Really? I didn't know that."

"Mom became a marine biologist because of Click," I add. "He's pretty special."

"Sounds like your mum was a pretty special too," she says.

"She was." It's the first time I've talked at any length about Mom since she died and I'm starting to get a little upset now, but there's one more thing I want to tell Alanna. She shared her story with me, so I want to share mine with her, all of it. I take a deep breath, then say, "She slipped on ice on the way back from the store and hit her head. She died before the ambulance arrived. Dad was with her, but I wish I had been too. Maybe if I'd been carrying the groceries instead of Mom… Or, at least, I'd have got to say goodbye." I'm crying now, so I have to stop talking.

"Oh, pet," Alanna says. "It's not your fault. It was just a terrible, horrible accident. If you have to blame something, blame the ice. It took my parents too. Stupid frozen water."

It's such a funny thing to say that I give a laugh and rub the tears from the corners of my eyes. Alanna puts her hand over mine, and we stay there for a while, staring out at the harbour. Sitting with Alanna makes me a little calmer until I remember about Cal and the others. Maybe Alanna will understand. I need to talk to someone about it or I think I'll crack up. Before I chicken out, I say, "Alanna, I've made a mess of everything."

She looks at me curiously. "What do you mean, pet?"

I tell her about the rapids and how I paddled off on my own. Then I explain what I'd said about Mattie's sea safari to Cal. "Cal doesn't want anything to do with me now," I say. "Neither do the others. I don't blame them. I've ruined their whole summer."

For a long while, Alanna is quiet. Finally she says, "Life can be tough, Rory. And we all make mistakes. Give Cal some time. He'll come around, they all will. Maybe you just need to talk to them, open up. Tell them what you told me about your mum when you feel able. In the meantime, I'm always here if you need a friend."

"Thanks, Alanna," I say. It's nice to know I have one friend on the island. Two, in fact: Alanna and Click.

Chapter 14

It's the next day and we've taken the RIB down to the harbour. I'm now sitting in it in my dive suit, watching Dad check the equipment for the hundredth time. First, he tests the air cylinders – we each wear one, a big yellow metal tank that's strapped to our backs. Mom always said that with the yellow cylinders and our black diving wetsuits, we look like underwater bumble-bees.

Next, Dad checks each regulator – the mouthpiece and tube attached to the cylinder. You breathe air in through the mouthpiece when you're underwater. There's a depth gauge on the regulator too, and also a gauge showing you how much air you have left in the cylinders.

Then Dad studies the masks, the buoyancy-control devices – or BCDs – which are basically vests that hold our tanks and also help us to control our depth underwater. Finally he presses some numbers into the dive computer on his wrist, which looks like a large watch.

"All set," he tells me. "And before you say it, yes, it did have to take so long. Safety is important, you know that. I've seen too many dive accidents to take short cuts."

"That's OK, I don't exactly have anywhere else to be." I sigh deeply.

"Less of the attitude, Rory. Let's try and enjoy ourselves today, yeah? Did you remember to pick up the food?"

"Oops."

Dad gives me a look.

"I'll go over for it now," I say. Dad asked Alanna to make us a picnic lunch. I was supposed to collect it earlier, while Dad was buying water in the shop.

"Did someone say food?" I look towards the harbour wall, where the voice came from, and there's Alanna, a large cool box in her hand.

"Careful, it's heavy," she says. The RIB is low in the water, so she has to bend down to pass the box to me.

"What's in there?" I ask, almost stumbling under the weight.

"Cake, sandwiches, fruit, lemonade, cookies, chocolate brownies. And a few other treats."

"Perfect," Dad says. "Is the cafe busy today, Alanna? Hope this wasn't too much trouble for you."

"No trouble at all," she says. "Mondays are usually quiet enough. I've taken the day off, in fact. Mollie and her nan are holding the fort. I need to collect some seaweed."

"For cooking?" I ask.

"You can cook with seaweed, all right, but, no, this time it's to make a natural face mask. Kelp and bladderwrack are great for detoxing the skin."

I look at her blankly.

She smiles and explains. "Kelp is a red seaweed and bladderwrack is brown, with air bubbles in it that keep it afloat," she says. "They're both full of fantastic oils and minerals that are great for the skin."

"But your skin's amazing already," I say.

"Thanks. It's not for me. I make herbal remedies for people and sell them over the Internet. Anyway, where are you guys off to? Looks like a pretty serious trip," she says, taking in Dad's underwater sound-recording equipment.

"I'm helping research a paper for a colleague at the moment," Dad says. "Measuring the echolocation range of bottlenose dolphins in the wild. So we thought we'd head out to Seafire Bay, see if we can't find ourselves a dolphin pod. Mattie says she spotted one out there yesterday. Or maybe we'll meet that Click fellow who helped us find you, Rory. Let's see who shows us their melon first."

Alanna looks at him curiously.

"Sorry," I say quickly. "It's a geeky in-joke. Dolphins have this special lump of tissue in their forehead called a melon. It controls their echolocation clicks."

"Echolocation, that's using sound to locate stuff, right?" Alanna says.

Dad nods eagerly. "A dolphin emits a click and it bounces off the object and then back to the dolphin, telling them if there are fish, or other dolphins, near by. Just like bats, only hundreds of times more complex. Did you know beluga whales can change the shape of their melon at will?"

Alanna smiles. "No, I didn't. Sounds fascinating."

"Oh, it is," Dad says, gabbling a little. He loves talking about his work. I'd find it annoying if I wasn't such a dolphin freak myself. "We," he continues, "marine biologists, that is, think cetaceans – sorry, sea mammals, like whales and dolphins – use the echolocation clicks to create images in their brains. Like the kind of pictures parents get of babies before they are born."

"The black-and-white pictures?" Alanna asks.

"Exactly," Dad says.

"Wow," Alanna says.

"They're amazing creatures," he says. "Tell me if I'm overloading you with information, Alanna. Dolphins are kind of our thing in this family, aren't they, Rory?"

I nod. That's an understatement. "Dolphins were Mom's life," I say to Alanna. "She was making this amazing dolphin dictionary. It meant everything to her." I'm hoping Dad is listening carefully. Maybe he'll change his mind about not working on it today. "Mom was determined to prove how smart dolphins really are, and how they have words for things just like we do. Dolphins' brains are actually way bigger than human ones."

"Rory's right," Dad says. "Margo was passionate about her research."

"That's why we have to finish it and publish it as soon as possible," I say.

"And we will," Dad says.

"Can't we try the D-com out today then? I'd love to see how it works underwater," I say.

"D-com?" asks Alanna.

"It's a computer Dad has been developing." I explain how Dad first made it to record dolphin sounds, but now we think we could play whistles back to them underwater. "It would be almost like we were talking to them." I turn back to Dad. "I know you haven't got it working yet, but don't give up! You have to keep trying. Maybe the computer is changing the dolphins' whistle frequency or something. That's why they don't understand the sounds."

Dad nods at me. "Smart, Rory. I think you may be right."

"Is the frequency really important then?" Alanna asks, looking a little confused.

"Sorry, Alanna," Dad says, "this really is nerdy science talk now. I hope we're not boring you. Want to fill her in, Rory, or will I?"

"You're the professor," I say.

"OK then, class," he begins with a smile. "Dolphins use different frequencies – the number of times that a sound is produced in a second – for different purposes. Lower frequencies – fewer repetitions per second – for social communication, and the higher-pitched noises for echolocation, so for finding fish and telling what shape or size a predator is."

"Their sonar," Alanna says. "Which comes from their melon, right?"

"You got it," Dad says. "And as Rory says, the D-Com may be distorting the frequency slightly, so the dolphins can't interpret the whistle we're playing them."

"Almost like we're not speaking the same language or something," I add. I think about this for a second. "Maybe you need to find a really smart dolphin who can work it out," I suggest.

"The Einstein of dolphins," Alanna says.

"Exactly!" I say.

Dad's quiet for a moment. "It's possible," he says finally. "The right dolphin might be able to translate the noise regardless of the frequency."

"You know what Einstein once said," Alanna says thoughtfully. "'Anyone who has never made a mistake has never tried anything new.' That was one of my dad's favourite quotes. He was a big Einstein fan. Maybe you need to make more mistakes, Aidan, not less. Maybe you need to try again. And keep trying until you prove your wife's theory."

Dad swallows. "That's a lot of maybes, Alanna." He blows out his breath in a rush, lifting his hair, and then stares out to sea. "Hey," he says, pointing at a dark shape on the horizon. "I think we've found our first bottlenose of the day. Hopefully he'll follow us out to the bay so we can dive with him."

"That's Click," I say. Click is definitely the cleverest dolphin I've ever met! "Dad, we should record some of Click's whistles and try playing them back to him with the D-Com. Maybe he'll be smart enough to figure it out, even if the frequency is wrong. Please? Can't we at least try?"

"Not today, Rory. The D-Com isn't set up and I have to do the echolocation work."

"But, Dad—" I say.

"Please, Rory, don't be difficult. I made a commitment, and I have to keep to it."

What about his commitment to Mom, though? I'm about to snap at him when Alanna says, "Well, it all sounds fascinating. I don't suppose you have room for a passenger? I'd love to come out with you, if it isn't too much trouble. Watch the scientists at work."

"Is there enough food for three?" Dad asks.

Alanna nods. "For an entire army. I went a bit overboard with the brownies. I know Rory likes them."

"OK with you to take a passenger, Rory?" Dad asks me.

It's more than OK with me – it's awesome. I was dreading being stuck with Dad on my own for hours, especially now he's refusing to work on the dolphin dictionary. "Yes! Totally," I say to Alanna. "Please come with us."

Dad laughs and hands Alanna a life jacket. "Welcome aboard, Alanna."

We motor out of the harbour and turn left, past a stretch of white sandy beach. Click follows a little distance behind, playing in the boat's frothy wake.

"That's Horseshoe Strand," Alanna tells Dad over the noise of the engine, pointing at the beach. "Great for swimming," she adds. It's the beach Cal and his friends took me to on my first day. My mood slumps as I remember that Cal is barely speaking to me.

"How are you feeling today, Rory?" Alanna asks. "Any better?"

Alanna and I are sitting on the small padded seat behind Dad, who's driving. We're so close that our shoulders are touching. Dad's eyes are fixed on the water, scanning it for more dolphins.

"I'm OK," I say.

"Good," she says and leaves it at that.

After a while, we pass a headland – called Seafire Point, according to Alanna – and Dad slows down to a stop but leaves the engine ticking over.

"This is Seafire Bay," he tells me, turning round. "Mattie says it's the safest place for diving. I'll move into the middle of the bay and we'll put down a diving line, Rory, and get into the water. Hopefully Click will stay around. And keep your eyes peeled for more dolphins, girls."

I nod at him. I know the routine off by heart. A buzz of adrenaline builds in my system, making my body tingle. I love swimming with dolphins – it's one of the best things in the whole world. They are such amazing swimmers. You can hear some of their echolocation clicks and communication whistles clearly when you're underwater – they can be pretty loud.

Mom's early research was all about identifying signature whistles. Each dolphin has its own one, like a fingerprint. They develop this when they're babies, like a human baby learning to say its name. And they can mimic each other's signature whistle too.

"Over there." Alanna points to her left, where a small dolphin pod is swimming in the distance, their grey backs curving out of the water. There's three of them, I think. Click has disappeared, though. That could mean there's a male in the pod. Male dolphins can be pretty aggressive towards other males, headbutting or ramming them, or even raking them with their teeth. Maybe Click feels threatened.

"Well spotted, Alanna," Dad says. "We'll move towards them slowly, and hopefully we won't scare them away." The boat creeps along at a snail's pace, and as soon as we get close to the dolphins, Dad cuts the engine and throws down the anchor.

"Ready to dive, Rory?" he asks me. We have to move quickly so we don't lose them.

I nod, feeling the adrenaline surge again.

"The hydrophone's set up," he says, "I just have to lower it into the water." The hydrophone is a microphone that can be used underwater. "I'll film the dolphins with my underwater camera while you swim with them, OK?"

"Sure." I'm still disappointed about Mom's research, but I'm itching to get into the water with the dolphins. I know it will cheer me up.

Dad looks at Alanna. "Are you happy to stay in the boat and watch?"

"More than happy," Alanna says. "It sounds fascinating. I can't believe you're part of all this cutting-edge research, Rory. Dolphin communication and now echolocation too. I'm really impressed. You're making scientific history, girl."

"I hadn't really thought about it like that. It's just Mom and Dad's work. I mean, it *was* their work. Before, you know. Now it's just Dad's work."

"It's part of your mum's legacy," Alanna says. "It's important research, Rory. I'm sure she'd be really pleased that you're both working on it together. You'll get back to the dolphin dictionary soon, I'm sure."

"Thanks," I say. I give her a smile.

Dad says nothing. I've noticed that he often goes quiet when people mention Mom. Just like I do sometimes. Or maybe it's guilt because of Alanna's comment about getting back to Mom's communication research.

He picks up his BCD vest and puts it on carefully, testing the two large clips at the front several times, clicking and unclicking them noisily.

"Dad!" I say "The clips are fine. Don't panic, OK?"

"Sorry, kiddo," he says. "Just some pre-dive nerves. Better get in the water or the dolphins will move on. You ready?"

"Yes, let's get wet." It's what Mom always said just before a dive.

He doesn't respond, but he's still fiddling with his BCD vest, so maybe he didn't hear me. Or maybe he's simply not listening.

Chapter 15

I love diving. It's so peaceful underwater. Once you roll backwards off the dive boat, the sea supports you, giving you a big wet hug. All you can hear is the gurgling of water in your ears, the bubbles escaping from your regulator as you breathe out, and when you're near the surface, the faint *boom, boom* of the waves slapping the side of the boat. And, if you're lucky, you can also hear the dolphins' whistles and clicks.

Dad swims beside me. We're swimming just under the surface of the water. When you're dive buddies, you have to stick together and look out for each other; it's one of the rules.

Dad stops and makes the diving signal for "OK" at me with one hand, his thumb and forefinger making a circle, the other three fingers upright, like a rabbit's head and ears. His other hand is holding an underwater camera. His hair is sticking up in a wavy spike and I can see his bright blue eyes through his mask. They're the opposite of Mom's eyes – hers were so dark brown they were almost black, like a seal's. Like mine.

After I've made the "OK" signal back to him, he points at the dolphin pod, which is swimming towards us to check us out. There are two adults and a baby.

I stay very still – only moving my dive fins a little to keep me near Dad – so I don't scare them away. The largest of the dolphins, the adult male, almost touches me as he swims past. At school, when I talk about swimming with dolphins, one of the first questions tends to be, "Are you not scared? What if one of them bites you?" Always the biting question! My school friends are as bad as Landy was about the seals. Dolphins, like seals, eat fish, not people. Plus, dolphins are super smart. They don't go around biting people for no reason.

"What does their skin feel like?" is usually the next question. And the truth is, it feels like cold, wet rubber. Like touching someone wearing a wetsuit, in fact.

Dad puts the camera to his eye and starts filming just as the second, smaller dolphin swims by me. I think that must be the adult female. She looks at me, and I smile to myself. I wonder what the dolphins make of us. Do they think we are another sea mammal? They never seem to be afraid and they are almost always friendly. Sometimes the dolphins who live by themselves can be a bit aggressive. Click isn't like that, of course. I wish he was here as well.

The adult female twists in a perfect circle and then dives deeper. I give Dad a thumbs down, indicating I want to descend, and he gives me another OK sign. I let the air out of my BCD, breathe out and sink further down in the water. Dad does the same. I point at the female dolphin to show Dad that I want to follow her and he gives another OK sign.

When she turns another somersault in the water, I copy her, but I'm much slower than she is. She makes an ultra-high whistle. It must be her signal for "play". I hope the hydrophone caught it and Dad got the corresponding body movements on his camera. Then I remember he's not studying communication today, just echolocation clicks – so the dolphin's body gestures and corresponding sounds are irrelevant. In fact, I'm not sure why he's filming me at all. This isn't Mom's research, this is different. Mom! I wish she was here with us now, diving with these dolphins. I start to feel sad and low, which is a terrible, wasteful way to feel when I'm swimming with these amazing creatures. I need to knock myself out of the doldrums with more dolphin playing.

I somersault again and then twist, corkscrewing my body three times, until I almost feel dizzy, and the female dolphin copies me. She's fast and elegant, cutting through the water like a knife. She gives another whistle, this time sounding even more excited. I think she likes me! The baby dolphin swims towards her then and rests her chin on her back. I bet the female is her mom. They look so comfortable together, so happy; it makes me feel happy too.

The adult dolphin – the dad, I reckon – joins them, nuzzling the baby with his beak. There are long, deep scars on his skin. It looks like he's been caught in a plastic fishing net and has fought his way out of it. Sometimes pieces of abandoned net end up in the ocean, and dolphins and other animals get tangled up in them.

Every year loads of dolphins get accidentally killed by fishermen, too. It's called by-catch. They get caught up in the mesh of the nets or in the ropes and can't break free. Dolphins need to breathe above water every ten to fifteen minutes, depending on the species. If they're caught underwater in nets for longer than that, they drown. Mom campaigned against the kinds of huge trawling nets that sweep up everything in the sea, including dolphins. They used to drive her crazy.

The baby dolphin has left her parents and is swimming slowly towards me. Even though she's young, she's still almost as long as I am, over four feet. Every now and then she looks back at her mom as if to say, "Can I play with her, Mom? Please?"

She spins round and whistles. I decide to name them: Scar, Dolphin Mom and Baby.

As Dad comes closer, still filming, I gently touch Baby's dorsal fin. When she doesn't seem to mind, I hold on tighter, and the next thing I know, she's pulling me along. I'm speeding through the water. She's so powerful, so strong, it's like flying.

"I think you made some new friends," Alanna says, after I'm back in the boat.

I smile. I'm so tired I can barely speak. Hanging onto Baby's dorsal fin used every muscle in my body, some of which I didn't know I had. Playing with dolphins is exhausting.

"I can't wait to see the video footage," Dad says, unclicking his BCD and taking it off before he puts the camera back in its case. "I thought Mattie and Cal might like to see you interacting with the dolphins, Rory. That's why I was filming you. The baby really took to you, kiddo. Watching you engaging with them was extraordinary. Alanna, will you come over and watch the footage with us later?"

"I'd love to – if that's OK with Rory." Alanna looks at me.

I nod again, still too pooped to speak.

Chapter 16

At eight o'clock that evening, we all settle down in Mattie's living room to watch Dad's dolphin footage. Mattie, Cal, Dad, Alanna and me.

Me, Mom and Dad used to watch hours of footage together after a dive.

Dad has set his laptop up on the coffee table and we're all gathered round it so we can see the screen. He's managed to link up some of the dolphins' sounds with the picture, even though in places it's a little out of sequence. "So this is the adult male bottlenose watching Rory," he narrates as we watch the video. The image on the screen shows me gliding through the water. Scar's eyes follow my movements.

"The clicking noises you're hearing is the dolphin scanning Rory with his echolocation clicks," Dad continues. "He can tell her size and weight from the clicks, but we're starting to think he can also tell what kind of mood she's in too – nervous, frightened, angry. Amazing, eh?"

"That is pretty incredible, Aidan," Mattie says.

"How long have you been diving, Rory?" Alanna asks.

"You're a natural."

"I did my first course when I was ten," I say. "I've always loved it. I did the advanced open water diver course last year."

"I did that course too, Mum, remember?" Cal says. "In Redrock last summer. It's no big deal."

"Cal." Mattie gives him a warning look and he slumps back into his chair, arms crossed against his chest. Alanna gives me a gentle smile.

"Click was about the size of that baby the first time Margo met him," Mattie says to me. "He was still with his pod then."

"What happened to them?" I ask her.

"I'm not exactly sure," she says. "There were five of them. Two females and three young dolphins, including Click. One day they were all swimming together in the bay, and the next thing the other four dolphins had disappeared. I guess we'll never know what happened to them. Click hasn't left the island since."

"Maybe he thinks they'll come back one day," I suggest. "And he's sticking around just in case."

"They're obviously dead," Cal says flatly.

"How would you know?" I snap.

"Rory!" Dad says.

I round on Dad. "Come on! It's a horrible thing to say."

"But realistic," Cal says.

"Cal!" Mattie warns him.

"Fine, OK," Cal says. "I get it. You can't handle the truth, Rory. They're not dead. They're living in fairyland – is that better?"

"Stop it, Cal," Mattie says and then gives a sigh. "Oh, Rory, love, I'm sorry to say it, but Cal is probably right. It's been nearly twenty years since they vanished. They're either dead or they simply abandoned him – it happens sometimes. Poor old Click. It must be lonely for him without his pod."

I say nothing, just stare down at the floor again. The room goes quiet.

Alanna touches my hand gently. Her skin feels cool. Mom's hands were always cold too. I teased her that she had dolphin skin.

"What are those markings on the larger dolphin's back, Rory?" Alanna asks, leaning towards the screen. "I bet you know."

"Scars from fishing nets," I say, glad the conversation has shifted. I don't like the thought of Click's family being dead *or* abandoning him. "Sometimes dolphins get caught up in the mesh. He's one of the lucky ones, he escaped."

"He is lucky," Mattie says. "They found some illegal gill nets off this island last summer. They were removed, but whoever put them there was never found. And up the coast, thirteen dolphins washed up dead on Achill Island around the same time. There were net marks on their bodies too. I've always wondered if they got caught in the gill nets and were then dumped in the sea."

Alanna looks shocked. "Really? That's terrible."

"It's a real problem," Dad agrees. "Margo was campaigning to get the nets modified so that they wouldn't trap dolphins.

She was really passionate about it. Fishing nets kill thousands of whales and dolphins every year."

There's silence for a moment, and then Dad points at the laptop. "And that's the dolphin mom, and the baby." On the screen, I see Baby swimming towards the version of me in the video. She nudges me with her beak, then she makes a rapid-fire, high-pitched whistle – *pop, pop, pop, pop*, just like corn popping in the microwave . She does it again: four high-pitched *pop*s.

"Do you hear her whistle?" I say. "It sounds like corn popping! I think that's her signature whistle. Our very own popcorn dolphin." Everyone except Cal laughs. "Hey, Dad, if you ever get the D-com working, we might be able to play her whistle back to her at the right frequency and she'll know we're saying her name."

"Really?" Mattie looks astonished. "Are we that close to communicating with dolphins? I knew your research was going well, Aidan, but I had no idea it was that advanced. How extraordinary."

Dad coughs a few times. "Um, well—"

"But Dad wants to spend his time on echolocation research instead," I say. "He wants to give up on Mom's work."

"Rory!" Dad says. "Please. We've talked about this. I explained that it's just not possible at the moment."

"Anything's possible if you want it badly enough, Dad," I say, jumping to my feet. "That's what Mom used to say. But you seem to have conveniently forgotten all about it."

And I walk out of the room and march towards the front door. Behind me I can hear Mattie say, "Leave her, Aidan. Let her walk it off. She'll cool down outside."

But she's wrong. I won't cool down about this, ever. Mom's research is so important and I don't understand why Dad won't finish it.

Chapter 17

I'm so angry and frustrated with Dad about Mom's research that I barely say a word to him over the next few days. Things aren't great in general, to be honest. Mattie's super busy and Cal still isn't speaking to me. I've been spending my time at the cafe with Alanna or swimming with Click in the harbour, anything to keep me away from Dad and Cal. In fact, if it wasn't for Click and Alanna, I'd be going crazy. Dad doesn't know about the swimming and Alanna's promised not to tell.

Alanna's been amazingly kind. She called into the house the other day and asked Dad if I could go kayaking with her. After all that business with Cal and the rescue and everything, Dad would probably have said no if I'd asked him.

"I'd love a kayaking buddy," she told him. "Go on, please, Aidan? We'll be really careful. And Rory needs to keep fit for her swimming. It's not good for her to be cooped up in the house all day."

"I don't want you taking any chances, Alanna," he said after reluctantly agreeing. "Don't go too far. Stay together and hug the coast, understand? And, Rory, take your cell phone. Put it in one of the waterproof cases."

Alanna smiled. "Thanks, Aidan. I'll look after Rory. I promise."

It was really fun – just the two of us paddling around the harbour with Click playing in the waves next to us.

On Thursday night, during dinner, Cal asks Dad if he can take the RIB out the following day. Mattie seems to have forgiven Cal for going kayaking in the rapids, or at least he's not grounded any more. Dad isn't keen at first.

"I don't know," he says. "There's a serious engine on that RIB, Cal. I'm not sure you could handle it alone."

"I have an advanced powerboat certificate," Cal says. "And I'll be careful, Aidan."

Cal's an expert at kayaking, diving *and* driving power boats? Typical. Is there anything he can't do? He's so darn accomplished it gets on my nerves.

"Mattie?" Dad looks at her. "What do you think? I'm just worried that the engine might fail or something. It's spluttering a bit."

Mattie gives a laugh. "I hate to say it, but that son of mine's a genius when it comes to fixing marine engines. How about he has a look at it for you before he goes out, Aidan? I bet he'll have it purring like a kitten in no time."

I roll my eyes. Of course he will.

"In fact," Mattie says, "why don't we all go out in the RIB

tomorrow? Rory can join us too. It's supposed to be a lovely day."

"I've arranged to go kayaking with Alanna," I say quickly. There's no way I want to be stuck on a boat with Cal and Dad all afternoon.

"We can meet you and Alanna in Seafire Bay, Rory," Dad says. "That way your old pops will get to spend some time with you."

I'll sound petty if I protest, so I say nothing. Cal's also gone pretty quiet.

"Great plan," Mattie says. "A Finn family outing. I can't wait."

The following afternoon, I meet Alanna on the small beach at the harbour. It's a beautiful day, warm and calm. The sea is glassy and inviting and I can't wait to get paddling.

"Talk about keen," she says, grinning at me. I'm already in my wetsuit and wetsuit boots, and my buoyancy aid is strapped on. My cell phone is zipped into the front of it. It has Mattie and Cal's numbers on it, just in case I can't get hold of Dad. Captain Careful is really living up to his name! The first time I went kayaking with Alanna, he wanted me to carry emergency flares until she reassured him that she wouldn't let me out of her sight. As it is, he has me carrying an extra rope and two spare paddles that I have to strap to each of the kayaks, just in case we lose our first paddle overboard.

Two kayaks are already at the water's edge, half pulled up

on the beach, the waves lapping at their bows. Mattie kindly dropped them off in her jeep earlier. Their black paddles are neatly propped against the harbour wall, like bars of a cage.

"I saw the gang heading out in the RIB a while back," Alanna says, pulling her wetsuit over her legs. "Your dad and Mattie and Cal."

"They want to meet us in Seafire Bay at four," I say. "Is that OK?" I'm not looking forward to seeing Cal and I'm almost hoping Alanna will say no and that she'd like to explore another part of the coastline instead, but, of course, she doesn't.

"Absolutely," she says. "That's a great idea. I hope the dolphins are still around. I'd love to see them again."

Once we're ready, Alanna shows me how to get into the kayak. It's a different kind to the ones I've used before, which are just a moulded piece of plastic you sit on and don't have a special built-in seat or hatches like this one. This is called a sea kayak and Alanna says they are better for exploring the coastline. You have to push this kayak into the sea and then get into it by putting one leg on either side. Following her lead, I lower my butt onto the top edge of the black seat, carefully, so the boat doesn't tip over. Then I swing my legs into the kayak, sticking them forwards until my feet reach the footrests, and then finally I wiggle my body down until I'm sitting on the seat. There's water in the bottom of the boat and on the seat and it soaks through my wetsuit, making my butt wet, but I don't mind. After paddling we'll probably go swimming, so I'll get wet anyway.

"Ready?" Alanna asks.

I nod firmly. "All set."

Alanna starts paddling out of the harbour and I follow her. The kayaks cut through the waves cleanly, like they're slicing the water apart. Once we're out on the open water, I feel a gentle sea breeze on my face. We turn left and start hugging the coast, paddling side by side.

I have a nice comfortable rhythm going, blade in and pull, opposite blade in and pull. I try to remember to "engage my core", as my swim coach would say, making my stomach muscles work. I miss swim training and my friends there, and I miss the adrenaline of competing. I can't wait to get back to it in the fall.

After a while, we pass Horseshoe Strand and start heading towards Seafire Point. I hear a splash beside me and look over. A familiar beak and head pop out of the water.

"Hey, Click," I say. He disappears for a second, then appears in front of my kayak again. I don't want to hit him, so I stop paddling. "What are you doing?" I ask. He's holding himself high out of the water, facing me, completely still. It's not normal dolphin behaviour. Usually they sweep past the side of boats or kayaks, swimming alongside or in the wake.

Alanna digs her paddle in vertically on one side, then the other, to make her kayak stop beside mine. "Why isn't he moving?" she asks me.

"I don't know," I say.

Click gives a long, low whistle with a higher pitch at the

end. I don't know what it means. It's not a whistle I've ever heard before. It's similar to the one dolphins in captivity make but with a different ending. He whistles again and then Alanna says, "Look, it's the RIB."

I spot an orange RIB powering towards us, Cal at the helm, Dad and Mattie sitting on the seat behind him. Cal slows the boat down as it approaches us, taking care to avoid Click. He comes to a clean stop beside us.

"Hey, girls," Mattie calls. "Want to come aboard?"

"Sure," Alanna says before I have a chance to say, "No, thanks, we're fine in the kayaks."

Mattie and Dad help us into the boat and Cal ties our kayaks behind the RIB.

Click is still close to us. He is holding half of his body out of the water, watching me. He dives down and, seconds later, leaps into the air, curving his body into an S shape. Then he swims towards the boat and stalls in the water just in front of us again.

"Why is Click staring at you like that?" Cal asks.

"I have no idea. Maybe he was telling us that you were approaching? But that doesn't make sense. You're here now and he's still doing it. There's clearly something else bothering him."

Click gives a whistle, then leaps into the air again, landing his S shape with a splash this time.

"Wow!" Alanna says. "I've never seen him do that before."

Click starts whistling again, this time four short, popping whistles in a row that sound like … popcorn.

I've heard that sound before, but…

Click is swimming away from us now, out to sea, but he keeps stopping and looking back.

"Looks like he wants us to follow him," Dad says.

I nod. Dad's right, but why is Click acting like this? It's so strange.

"Hey," Mattie says, pointing at the water near where Click is swimming. "There's something… What *is* that?"

Cal scans the water. "Yellow marker buoys. You can just about make them out under the waves. They're probably holding up a fishing net."

"But Click's swimming towards it! He might get caught, especially if he keeps looking back at us," I say. "I don't understand what's going on, but, Dad, we have to do something!" Just then Click ducks down under the water and out of sight. "Dad! He's disappeared. What if he gets stuck?"

"What are we going to do?" Alanna asks. "Call the coastguard?"

"No," Mattie says. "That would take too long. Click could get into trouble before then."

"How long can dolphins stay underwater?" Alanna asks.

"Ten minutes. Maybe a bit longer," Dad says. "Can the nets be pulled up?"

"No, they're usually fixed to the sea bed," Mattie says.

"So we have to go down and stop Click," I say. "We have to dive. It's the only way to check that Click is OK. Please, Dad."

Mattie looks at Dad. "Aidan?"

"Rory's right," he says. "I'll have to dive. Hopefully it's not too late."

"You can't go down on your own, Dad," I say. "I'll go with you."

"No, I'm sorry, Rory," he says. "I can't let you do that. Wild dolphins can be unpredictable when they're stressed, and if Click does get stuck in that netting, there's no knowing how he'll react. Also that other pod might be here somewhere."

The other pod… And then I remember – Click's whistle was from Mom's research.

"Danger," I say. "Click's whistle. It means danger. It was in Mom's dolphin dictionary, the one she started when she was younger. He was telling us about the fishing nets."

"You're exactly right, Rory," Dad says. "I should have thought of that. But why warn us and then swim towards them?"

"I bet one of the other dolphins is stuck in the net!" I say suddenly. "The mom or the baby." Then I remember the other noise Click made – the pop-pop-popping sound. "He was making the baby dolphin's signature whistle!" I say. "He was trying to tell us that Baby is in trouble. Maybe she's caught in the net!"

"If that's what Click was doing, that would be … *incredible*," Mattie says.

"You're right," Dad says. "It would. And if that is the case, then the other pod will be around here and there is even more reason for you to stay on the boat, Rory. That male is big. And the mother could be there too. One of them could accidentally hit you with their tail, give you concussion, knock out your air supply, maybe even bite you. I'm sorry, but it's just not—"

"Dad, those dolphins won't hurt me, I know it. I'm begging you, Dad, please? Let me do this with you. I know you're scared something will happen to me, that I'll have an accident like Mom, but nothing's going to go wrong, I swear." I pause and then add, "Mom wouldn't want you to dive alone. She'd want us to do it together."

He goes quiet. Then he gives a long, deep sigh. "I don't like this and it goes against all my instincts, but you're right, she would. You can dive with me. But dive safe and don't take any risks."

"Thanks, Dad."

"I'm coming too," Cal says. "If the baby is caught in the nets, you'll need help to cut her out."

"OK," Dad says. "You're on, Cal. Let's dive."

Chapter 18

I'm sitting on the side of the RIB, looking at Dad and Cal. We all have our BCDs on, tanks on our backs and fins on our feet. We also have dive knives strapped to our calves. Bare calf in Cal's case – he's still in his swimming shorts and a rash vest, but it will have to do. There's no dive suit for him.

Mattie and Alanna are in the boat, watching us. They both look worried, but I know they understand why we have to dive.

"Let's get wet," Cal says.

A shiver runs up my spine. It's what Mom always used to say before a dive... How does he—? But there's no time to think about it. I nod at Cal and then at Dad. "Let's get wet," I murmur. After pulling my dive mask over my face and fixing the regulator in my mouth, I do a backwards roll off the dive boat and hit the water with a splash. Cal's just behind me, followed by Dad. I give them an OK sign and then a thumbs down, descend sign. They nod, return my thumbs down and we all let the air out of our BCDs and slip under the surface together.

The first thing I see is Click hovering in the water, as if he's waiting for us. He swims away from us and then turns to check we're still behind him. We follow his tail flukes. After diving for several metres, he starts to move horizontally until there's a faint shimmer in the water ahead of us. As we draw closer, I see that it's a large gill net. There are lots of fish inside – some of them are still struggling but many are dead. And then I spot Baby. We were right – she is stuck in the net. Her tail flukes are both caught in the mesh and she's making tiny squawking noises, clearly terrified. Scar is pulling at the net, trying to free her. Dolphin Mom's trapped too, just below Baby, but unlike her little one, she's still.

Click turns his head as if to say, "Please help her."

I swim towards the net. There's a moment when I'm scared Scar will attack me – he turns round so fast – but then Click gives a whistle and Scar moves away. I take my knife out of its holder and start slashing at the plastic to try and free Baby. Cal and Dad do the same, and within seconds, Baby is free! She floats away from the net, motionless. But as we watch, her tail twitches, followed by her flippers, and then suddenly she comes to life. She's sluggish, but she manages to swim towards the surface to breathe, Scar by her side. Baby's going to survive! Cal gives me an OK sign and I give him one back. But it's not over yet – Dolphin Mom is still trapped. I point at her and Cal nods. Dad is way ahead of us, though, and has already swum over to her, his knife outstretched.

Click follows him and starts whistling at Dolphin Mom.

I think he's telling her that we've come to help, that she's going to be all right now.

She's struggled so much that the mesh is wrapped around her whole body, along with one of the ropes that holds the side of the net. I point at the rope and then at Dad. He nods and gets to work hacking through the thick twist of blue plastic.

I start cutting Dolphin Mom out of the net, beginning at her beak. Cal helps me. Her eyes are open, but they look dull and listless. I think she can sense me because her eyelids are flickering a little, but she's not moving. It's not looking good.

I saw at the net as quickly as I can, cursing the fishermen who put her in this danger. What were they thinking? Idiots! But I can't dwell on that right now. I have to keep cutting. I attack the mesh harder, cutting and pulling, cutting and pulling. The plastic is sharp and it eats through the flesh on my fingers as I try to reef it away from her tail flukes. I spot wafts of blood in the water – my blood! Cal is working equally hard.

Click stays right beside us, watching our work. After a few frantic minutes, the mesh comes apart and Dolphin Mom floats free of her horrible plastic chains. But unlike Baby, she's not moving her tail or her fins.

Come on, I urge her, *swim! Baby needs you. You can't die. You can't leave her alone in the world.* But it's no use – Dolphin Mom's still and her eyes are closed.

Cal puts his hand on my arm and makes the thumbs up sign. He wants to surface.

I shake my head and point at Dolphin Mom. He hugs himself and gestures upwards again. Of course – without a wetsuit, he must be freezing. The water down here is icy cold. He needs to surface, and as his dive buddy, I have to go with him. *I have to leave you,* I tell Dolphin Mom. We signal to Dad and all surface, together.

When we get back up, Cal is almost blue with the cold. He's shivering violently and his teeth are chattering so much he can't talk.

"Cal!" Mattie says from the boat. "Are you all right?"

I pull out my regulator. "He's freezing," I tell her and Alanna. "There's a survival blanket in one of the boxes. Get him into the boat and wrap it around him."

"Will do," Alanna says. They pull him into the dive boat, take off his diving gear, place him carefully on the floor and wrap the silver foil blanket around his shaking body.

"Did you see Baby?" I ask Alanna when I'm sitting in the RIB. "She came up to breathe, right?"

"We saw her," Alanna says.

"What about the mom?" Dad asks. "She was trapped in the net too."

Alanna shakes her head and I feel hollow inside.

"Then she didn't make it," I say. "We should have split up. Or freed her first. I'm so stupid. I saw that she wasn't moving and her eyes were closing over, but I still went to Baby first. The mom must have been trapped down there a lot longer, though. We should have cut her loose first. But we helped Baby instead." Hot tears start to roll down my cheeks. I wipe them away and stare down at the floor, willing myself to stop crying. "She's dead because of me."

"Babies have smaller lungs," Dad says. "We were right to free the baby first, Rory. Listen to me, it's not your fault." He puts his arm around me, but I shrug it off.

"But she's dead!" I practically shout, my head still down. "I drowned her. She was relying on me and I failed."

"No, Rory, it's my fault," he says. "If only I'd said yes to you diving with me sooner. If I'd trusted you—"

Mattie cuts in. "It's no one's fault except those stupid fishermen. I can't believe they're still laying those killer nets. It's completely illegal so close to the shore. I'm ringing the coastguard right now and I hope they find them and lock them up. Murderers."

"Mattie's right," Alanna says. "You did your best, Rory. I think you and Cal and your dad are heroes."

At that I start to cry again. If I'm such a hero, why do I feel so miserable?

I hear a splash in the water behind me and I swing around. It's Scar, followed by Baby.

"Would you look who's come up to say hello," Dad says.

Baby's right fluke is bleeding, leaving red swirls in the water.

"Is she going to be OK, Dad?" I ask. "That cut looks pretty bad. It must hurt." I sliced my hands on the nets too and they are stinging like crazy. I ball them tightly, which helps a little.

"It's not too deep," Dad says after studying the wound on Baby's fluke for a few seconds. "It'll heal up quickly, although she'll have quite a scar, like her dad. She's going to be just fine. Hey, what's that?" He points at a dark shape moving under the surface. And I know immediately what it is – Dolphin Mom's body. Click is there too. He's lifting her up and forcing her head into the air.

"What's Click up to?" Mattie asks Dad. "I've never seen a dolphin do that before. Click really is amazing."

Dad is so transfixed he doesn't answer for a second. "Margo said she witnessed it once, but I didn't believe her. Click's trying to get her to breathe. Look at her blowhole. Is it my imagination or is the membrane starting to move?"

Dad's right. The membrane is opening. She's still alive! But does she have the energy to take a breath?

Go on, Dolphin Mom, I will her. *Take a breath. Do it for Baby.*

Water splutters out of her blowhole and her head twitches.

"Looks like she's coming to," Mattie says. "Come on, girl, you can do it. Breathe. Cal, you have to see this. Aidan, will you help him up?"

Dad helps Cal stagger to his feet. Still wrapped in his silver cocoon, Cal stands at the edge of the RIB and stares down at Dolphin Mom. "C-c-come on, g-girl," his says, his voice ragged but getting stronger.

And then Dolphin Mom blows more water out of her blow hole, takes a breath and opens her eyes.

"Yes!" Dad says, punching the air. Then he hugs me. "She's alive, kiddo." His eyes are sparkling. "You did it."

"*We* did it," I point out. I'm so full of relief and happiness I could float off like a helium balloon. "Together. You, me and Cal." I catch Cal's gaze and he nods at me, but he doesn't smile. So it's like that, is it? Back to normal. I slump a little, feeling sad. After everything that's happened today, I thought we'd be friends. Clearly not. Deflated, I try to concentrate on Dolphin Mom instead.

Her body goes from being limp and defeated to strong and powerful. She gives a few flicks of her tail, as if testing it still works, and then dives. Seconds later she leaps out of the water in a graceful arc, splashing us all as she lands. It's as if she's saying, "Look at me, I'm alive. I'm alive!"

The next time she jumps, Scar, Baby and Click leap with her. Scar throws in a spin, twisting his body at speed and landing so perfectly in the water he barely makes a ripple.

Then Dolphin Mom pops up again just in front of me. She gives one last whistle before diving again to join her family and Click.

"If I didn't know better," Alanna says to me, "I'd say that dolphin just said thank you."

I smile at Alanna. That's exactly what I was thinking.

Chapter 19

While Dad and Mattie put the RIB back onto its trailer and pull it out of the water with the jeep, Cal lies across the back seats getting warm and I walk to the cafe with Alanna to fetch hot sugary tea for everyone. Alanna says it's good for cold and shock.

"It meant a lot to you, saving those dolphins, didn't it?" Alanna asks me as she pops some brownies into a container to go with the tea. "You have a special bond with them. Mattie says your mum was just the same."

I shrug.

"It's hard, isn't it? Talking about her. That feeling will pass," Alanna says, reading my mind. "One day you'll be able to talk about her without being sad." Her green eyes are soft and warm.

"I talk to her in my head sometimes," I admit. "It makes me feel closer to her. Like she's still here."

Alanna smiles gently. "And she is still here, looking over you and making sure you're safe. She'll always be with you." Alanna places her hand on her chest. "In here. In your heart.

And you're lucky – you still have your dad to look out for you."

"I know, but I'm not as close to Dad. It's not like me and Mom. And he never lets me do anything any more. Since Mom's accident, it's like he's scared of the whole world. But I want to feel free. I want to swim and dive and maybe study dolphins, like Mom did. I don't want to worry all the time."

"How's that tea coming along?" Mattie sticks her head around the kitchen door. "I'm gasping for a cuppa."

"Be there in a second." Alanna puts her hand over mine and says in a low voice, "He's trying to protect you, Rory. He loves you more than anything. I think he's hurting just as much as you are. And he worries about you – which makes him overly cautious. Talk to him about your mum and about how you're feeling. Give him a chance."

As soon as we get back to Harbour Cottage, Mattie runs a hot bath for Cal, who is looking less like a ghost but still shivering. Dad disappears into his room to change.

After taking a shower – and, boy, did I need one – I go into the kitchen to get a glass of water. Mattie's sitting at the kitchen table, cradling a mug in her hands. She smiles up at me. "I've just made some hot chocolate." She nods at a saucepan on the stove. "Would you like some? I have marshmallows."

"Sure, sounds good," I say with a smile.

She pours me a mug and hands it over. "Sit down and join me. There's something I'd like to tell you." Mattie looks sad.

"Is Cal going to be all right?" I ask, suddenly anxious. Maybe he has hypothermia or something.

"He'll be fine. He's a strong lad. Don't be worrying about him. But that is what I wanted to talk to you about – you and Cal. Well, more specifically about family." She runs her finger along the rim of her mug. "I wish I'd kept in better touch with your mum after she moved to New York, but it wasn't as easy as it is now and we were busy being teenagers. The day your mum contacted me was one of the happiest days of my life, and I don't say that lightly. We emailed each other for a while and then she rang me. It was like the years just melted away and we were two teenagers again, laughing and being silly."

Mattie shifts in her chair. "When she said she was planning to visit Ireland with you and your dad, I was so excited. I couldn't wait to see her. We made so many plans. We'd go swimming every morning on Horseshoe Strand, go kayaking at night and see the phosphorescence around Seafire Bay, go dolphin- and whale-watching … all kinds of things." Mattie presses her lips together, clearly upset. "And then your poor dad had to ring me and break the news about her … you know. I was devastated." She takes a deep breath, her eyes welling up. "I couldn't believe I'd never get to see her again. And I was so angry with myself too. I lost all those years with her. Years we could have spent together."

She leans forwards, her voice urgent. "Rory, don't let the same thing happen to you and Cal. My boy is as stubborn as they come, I know that. But he's a good lad, and you two could be great friends if you'd only let him in."

"But he hates me," I say.

Mattie takes one of my hands. Her skin is warm. "He doesn't hate you, I promise. Just try talking to him. Please? For me and for your mum. Just before she died, she said something to me – I'll never forget it. She said, 'You know, Mattie, we're better than friends – we're family. And family is for ever.' Family meant everything to her, along with her beloved dolphins."

Now I start to cry. "But I know he hates me and he has every right to. I said some really awful things and I've ruined his summer."

"I don't hate you." I turn round to find Cal standing in the open doorway.

Mattie hands me a tissue and I mop up my tears. "You must think I'm such a dork, crying like a baby," I say, embarrassed.

"No," he says. "I think you're really brave. You cut your hands to shreds on that fishing net, but you kept going. You were amazing. You saved those dolphins! You worked out what Click was trying to tell you and you saved them. If it wasn't for you, they'd be dead."

"You helped too, Cal. We did it together."

"It really is extraordinary," Mattie says. "You communicated with a dolphin, Rory. A dolphin in a million. You know what this means? Your parents' research is bang on track. And maybe Click will be able to prove it. You have to get your dad to work with Click."

I smile at her. "I know, right? Will you help me persuade him, Mattie?"

"If he needs persuading then, yes, I will," Mattie says. "I promise. Us Finn women have to stick together."

"Thanks, Mattie," I say, grateful for her support.

"I can talk to him too, if you like," Cal says. "Mum's right – your dad should definitely study Click."

"Thanks. Cal, can I ask you something? Just before we were diving you said, 'Let's get wet.' Why?"

He shrugs. "It's something Mum always says before she gets in the water."

"Same with my mom. She used to, I mean." I give him a tentative smile.

He smiles back. "Look, can we start again, Rory?" he asks. "I'm sorry if I've been mean to you. Friends?"

Mattie was right when she said that family is important, and it would have meant such a lot to Mom to know that me and Cal were close, so I nod and say, "Friends. And family too, which is even better. Right, Mattie?"

"Oh, Rory." Mattie's eyes well up again, setting me off.

"What are you two crying about?" Cal looks at us, baffled. "Girls! You're all insane. You know that, don't you?"

Mattie and I splutter with laughter through our tears.

That night, although I'm still physically exhausted from the dive, I can't sleep. Mattie dressed and bandaged up my hands earlier, but they still throb when I try to move them or to wiggle my fingers. She said I was lucky – I could have severed a nerve or something – but they will take time to heal.

I lie there, mulling over what happened today and thinking about Click, Dolphin Mom and Baby, and then my own mom. I know she'd be proud of me for saving those dolphins' lives. She'd be proud of Cal, too. I wish she'd gotten to meet him and to spend time with us all on the island – her dolphin-loving Irish and American family.

I lie still for a few more minutes, before sitting up in bed and switching on my light. Then I open the drawer on my bedside table and take out Mom's dolphin journal. I begin to write.

Friday 10 July

Dear Mom,

I saved two dolphins today – but you know that, don't you? You were there with me, watching over me, making sure I was safe.

Alanna says you'll always be with me – that you'll live for ever in my heart, and I know it's the truth. I hope I'm in yours too.

Mom, you were right all along. Dolphins do name things and talk to each other. They can do it with us too, if we listen and watch hard enough. Click whistled "Danger" at me today and linked it with the baby dolphin's name – "Popcorn". He "talked" to me.

I wish you were here. You could tell all those stuffy people who didn't believe you that they were wrong. Dolphins are super smart and deserve our respect.

Are there dolphins where you are now, Mom? I hope so.

I miss you so much. And Mattie misses you, and Dad misses you. It makes me sad to think that there are so many things you'll never get to do. Mattie told me about all the cool stuff you two had planned for the summer. I'm sure you and Dad had your own plans. And we had plans too, didn't we? For our Mom and Rory trips in the future. Loads of travel plans, and not all dolphin linked either - visiting Paris together. Going up the Eiffel Tower, seeing the Mona Lisa. New York, Rome, Iceland ... but none of that is ever going to happen now.

But I was thinking, maybe I could do some of those things with Dad instead. And you'd be there too, because you'd be watching me. I can stand on the top of the Eiffel Tower with Pops and send you my love and you'll feel me, thinking about you and loving you.

Always,
Aurora XXX

P.S. One day I'm going to work with dolphins, just like you. Watch this space...

Chapter 20

I feel groggy the following morning. I didn't fall asleep until after midnight. My arms and shoulders are stiff from all the paddling and diving and my hands are stinging under the dressings. I take a shower, letting the warm water fall onto my skin and massage my muscles.

I pull on some sweatpants and a top and then I pull back the curtains at the French doors to see what sort of day it is outside. It's a bright, sunny one. There are a couple of fluffy clouds scudding past, but it's pretty clear. I give a start when I see a man staring out to sea with a pair of binoculars – but it's only Dad.

I open the doors and step outside, the flagstones of the patio cold under my bare feet.

"Sorry, kiddo, I didn't mean to startle you," he says.

"What are you doing out here?" I ask him.

"Seeing if I can spot the dolphin pod," he says, "and thinking about your mom. Sorry, I know you find it hard to talk about her." He pats the seat beside him. "Care to join your old pops?"

I shrug. "Okey-dokey, kiddo," I say.

He gives a gentle laugh.

I sit down. Then I put my feet on the wooden seat, fold my legs in front of me and hug them against my chest with my arms. I rest my chin on my knees.

We sit there in silence for a few minutes, gazing out at the sea.

"Beautiful, isn't it?" Dad says.

"Yes," I murmur. From here you can see glossy green fields, the golden yellow curve of Horseshoe Strand and all the way across to Seafire Bay, where the sun is dancing on the tips of the waves.

"Any sign of the dolphins?" I ask him.

"No. But I haven't been here long." He turns and looks at me. "I was talking to Mattie and Cal over breakfast. They want us to extend our trip so I can study Click. They think he might be able to help with my research. After what happened yesterday, when he communicated with you like that and then showed us where to find the baby dolphin, I think they may be right. I'm not teaching again until September, so the university won't mind if I'm not in Stony Brook for a while. How would you feel about staying until the end of the summer? I know you're eager to get home and to see your friends and Magda, and if you don't want to—"

I cut him off. "Seriously? Yes, I absolutely want to! Does this mean you're going back to Mom's research?"

"Yes, I think so. Rory, I've found the last six months without your mom almost unbearable. I had to distance myself from the work we did together – it just reminded me of her too much. Every time I saw her handwriting or watched the videos of her dives or heard her voice…" He tails off. "I couldn't deal with it. That's why I agreed to work on the echolocation project for a while, not because I don't believe in your mom's work or don't want to finish it. Do you understand? I just found it so darn hard. It's getting a little easier now, and being here with Mattie and being able to talk to her about Margo is helping."

I can't talk because there's a lump in my throat. I nod instead. All my anger and frustration at him is melting away. Poor Dad, I've been pretty tough on him. I take a few deep breaths. "I'm sorry, Dad," I say quietly. "I just thought you didn't want to do the research, not that you couldn't. Alanna said I shouldn't be so hard on you. I've been talking to her a bit too, about Mom and the accident and everything."

"I'm so happy you've found a friend here," Dad says. "Someone special to talk to. I know I've been too caught up in my own thoughts to be much use. It can't have been easy for you, especially with me worrying all the time."

"I know you're trying to protect me because of what happened to Mom, but you can't protect me from the whole world," I say. "You've got to let me live."

"I know that I have to stop wrapping you in cotton wool, Rory, honest I do. It's just so difficult. Since your mum died, I've been feeling more and more anxious. Margo was the fun one – she was fearless. It was my job to keep her safe and support all her mad schemes. While she went off diving, I stayed in the lab and built up the database. We were a good team. But in the end I couldn't keep her safe. I was right beside her, but I couldn't save her. I loved her so much, but it didn't make any difference – she still died."

"It wasn't your fault, Dad. And it wasn't my fault for not being there to carry the groceries. I realize that now."

"Oh, Rory, is that what you've been thinking? No!"

"It's OK. I know it wasn't anyone's fault. Alanna said if we have to blame something, we should blame the stupid ice, not ourselves." I take a deep breath. There's something I have to tell him and it's not going to be easy. "I was really angry with Mom for leaving me. I know it's terrible and I don't feel like that now, but I did."

Dad sighs. "I hear you, Rory. I was angry too, not with your mom, but with the world for allowing something so awful to happen to our family. But I guess I'm starting to accept things now. Margo's not coming back and we have to learn to live without her."

"I know," I say. "But it's so hard. For Mattie too. I was talking to her last night. She and Mom had all these things they wanted to do together, like midnight kayaking. Did she tell you about them?"

"Yes. We've talked a lot over the last few days. Your mom always had a ton of plans. There were so many things she wanted to do, places she wanted to see. Remember all your mom and Rory trips? Made me feel pretty left out, to be honest."

I unfold my legs and then bump him with my shoulder, something I haven't done for a long time. "Sorry," I say.

"It's OK," he says. "Your mom loved those days. They meant a lot to her. She wanted the world for you, kiddo. I'm sure, wherever she is, she still does." He blows out his breath and stares out to sea again. "Sorry, I'm talking about her again. I'll stop now."

"No," I say. "Don't stop. I want to be able to talk about her, remember her. I miss her."

"Me too, kiddo. Me too. But life goes on, I guess, and she'd want us both to be happy. We have to give it a shot, to try and be a family together, just the two of us. Maybe we can put the last six months behind us and start again? What do you think?"

Dad's right – Mom would definitely want us to be happy. "We can try." Then I think of something else. "Can Mattie and Cal come and stay with us in Stony Brook sometime? When we go back. I think Mom would like that."

"Great idea." He gives me a smile.

"And maybe we can continue some of Mom's research together? Your D-Com is genius. I want to know more about it."

He looks surprised. "Really? I didn't think you'd be interested in the D-Com side of things. Isn't it a bit geeky?"

"An underwater computer that can help us communicate with dolphins? Are you kidding? It's so radical it makes my brain hurt just thinking about it. I'm sorry I didn't say it before.

I was a bit annoyed with you about the whole echolocation thing."

He grins. "That's OK, and I guess the D-com is a bit *radical*. And, you know something, don't tell anyone, but the echolocation research is pretty boring."

I laugh. "I won't tell any of your marine biology friends, don't worry. Hey, maybe we could have a Dad and Rory day tomorrow. Take the boat out to Seafire Bay. See how Scar and Dolphin Mom and Baby are doing. Work with Click and the D-Com."

"I'd love that, Aurora." He twists around and holds out his arms to me. I hesitate for a second. I haven't let Dad hug me properly since Mom died, but it's time. I fall into his arms and hug him back.

Epilogue

Three Years Later
The Irish Times, 21 August

Groundbreaking Dolphin Discovery Made in Irish Waters

Father-and-daughter team Professor Aidan Kinsella of North Shore University, Stony Brook, USA, and Aurora Finn-Kinsella made history yesterday when they successfully undertook two-way communication with a bottlenose dolphin in the waters around Little Bird Island, off the coast of West Cork, Ireland.

The D-com – a cutting-edge computer developed by Professor Kinsella with his late wife Professor Margo Finn – can be used underwater to generate artificial "dolphin" whistles that the mammals can understand and respond to. To date, the research, involving a dolphin that locals call "Click", has been limited to asking Click to collect a piece of seaweed and pass it to Aurora. The D-com has created a signature whistle that Click has learned to associate with Aurora.

The game changer came when Click made the whistle for Aurora's name and the D-com was able to recognize it.

Speaking about the breakthrough, Professor Kinsella said: "It's taken us three long years to get here, and it wouldn't have happened without the outstanding work undertaken by my wife. We will be publishing her research in the fall, and dolphin lovers all over the world will be able to read about her extraordinary work and her extraordinary life. We believe that dolphins are one of the most intelligent species on the planet and deserve our respect and our protection. Aurora and I are proud to be continuing Margo's work. Together."

Five things you might not know about me

by Rory Kinsella

1. My favourite animal is the bottlenose dolphin.
(In fact, you probably do know this! ☺)

2. I've watched the movie *A Dolphin's Tale* six times
and counting. It's based on the true story of Winter,
a bottlenose dolphin who lost her tail after getting
entangled in a fishing line. She was rescued off the
Florida coast and was fitted with a prosthetic tail.
If you haven't watched it, do – it's amazing.

3. I *love* chocolate brownies.
My mom made the most delicious ones.

4. My favourite colour (or color, as we spell it in
the US) is … can you guess? … yes, *sea* blue!

5. Aurora means "dawn". It was my mom's
favourite time of the day and she said having me
was like the sun coming up. ☺

A Very Special Chocolate Brownie Recipe

from Rory's Mom, Margo

Ingredients (*makes 9 large brownies*)

100g dark chocolate, grated or chopped finely
125g butter
75g self-raising flour
275g caster sugar
2 eggs, beaten lightly
½ teaspoon vanilla essence
2 tablespoons cocoa powder

Instructions

1. Ask a parent or guardian to preheat the
oven to 160°C for a fan oven or 180°C for a normal
oven or gas mark 4.

2. Cut a piece of baking parchment and place it on the baking tray.

3. Place the grated or chopped chocolate in a heatproof bowl over a saucepan of hot water. Make sure no water goes into the chocolate! Ask an adult to help you with this part as it can be tricky. Stir the chocolate gently until it has melted.

4. Place the butter, sugar and vanilla in a large mixing bowl and beat until soft. Add the lightly beaten eggs gradually, mixing them in as you go.

5. Add all the flour and cocoa powder. Then pour in the melted chocolate carefully and mix everything all together.

6. Transfer the mixture into the baking tin and smooth it down with the back of a spoon.

7. Place the tray in the oven and bake for 30 to 35 minutes. The brownies should be soft in the middle, with a crispy top. Get an adult to help you with the oven and be careful because it will be hot!

8. Allow the brownies to cool in the baking tray and then cut them into squares.

Warm brownies are delicious with ice cream.
Enjoy!

How much do you know about dolphins and whales? Try this fun quiz and see!

(Answers at the end)

1. Which animals are whales and dolphins most closely related to?
   a. Crocodiles
   b. Hoofed mammals like hippos
   c. Elephants

2. How far can a humpback whale's song travel?
   a. 100 km
   b. 1,000 km
   c. 10,000 km

3. What is the largest animal that has ever lived on earth?
   a. Fin whale
   b. Tyrannosaurus Rex
   c. Blue whale

4. Can dolphins drown?
   a. Yes
   b. No

5. How do dolphins sleep?

    a. They curl up on the sea bed.

    b. They float on top of the water.

    c. They shut down half their brain.

1. The answer is b. A lot of people answer "elephants", but dolphins and whales are, in fact, most closely related to hippos.

2. The answer is c. The sound can take eight hours to travel this distance.

3. The answer is c. The blue whale can weigh up to 170 tonnes, which is the same weight as thirty African elephants. The Tyrannosaurus Rex only weighed seven tonnes.

4. The answer is a. Like all mammals, whales and dolphins have to breathe air. Whales can stay underwater for up to 90 minutes. Dolphins need to breathe every 10 or 15 minutes.

5. The answer is c. Dolphins have to be conscious (awake) to breath. This means that they cannot go into a full deep sleep, so instead they shut down half their brain. This is called unihemispheric sleeping.

Acknowledgements

I'm very grateful to the team at Walker Books, who do all the hard work behind the scenes: my wonderful editors, Annalie and Emily; Maria, who designed the beautiful cover, which is one of my all-time favourites; and Jack, who drew the map of Little Bird Island. Thanks also to all those on the sales and marketing side, especially Conor in Ireland, Jo, Jill, Sarah, Heidi and the team.

My agents, Philippa and Peta, are always a joy to work with and keep me smiling. And to my friends in the children's book world, especially the gang in Dubray, Eason, Gutter, Hodges Figgis, Raven and Bridge Street Books. You are all so dedicated to the cause – I salute you! Also to the teams at Children's Books Ireland, the Irish Writers Centre, Mountains to Sea Book Festival and Listowel Writers Week – all Trojan children's book lovers.

My family and friends keep me sane and put up with my odd working hours and festival trips – thanks, all of you!

I had some very special help with this book. Jasmine Hutchinson and the Orville A. Todd Book Club of Spackenkill, Poughkeepsie, New York, read the manuscript and made some great suggestions. Also the tireless Kathryne Alfred Del Sesto picked through the chapters and made sure Rory sounded like an authentic American teenager.

My writer friend Kate Thompson and her husband, Malcom Douglas, helped with the diving scenes, and I'm most grateful for their expertise. Wildlife expert Don Conroy was also so kind and helpful.

Finally, I'd like to thank a woman I've never met. Denise Herzing has been working with dolphins for over 28 years. Watching her TED talk about her work inspired me to find out more about dolphin communication. When I was a young girl, I wanted to be a marine biologist, and through writing this book, I've been able to live my dream in a small way.

My final thanks are to you – the reader of this book. Thank you for picking up my novel. If you liked Rory's story, I'd love to hear from you. Drop me a line – sarah@sarahwebb.ie.

Yours in books,
Sarah XXX

Sarah Webb worked as a children's bookseller for many years before becoming a full-time writer. Writing is her dream job because it means she can travel, read books and magazines, watch movies, and interrogate friends and family, all in the name of "research". She adores stationery, especially stickers, and is a huge reader – she reads at least one book a week. As well as The Songbird Cafe Girls series, Sarah has written six Ask Amy Green books, eleven adult novels and many books for younger children. She visits a school every Friday during term time and loves meeting young readers and writers. She has been shortlisted for the Queen of Teen Award (twice!) and the Irish Book Awards.

Find out more about Sarah at www.SarahWebb.ie or on Twitter (@sarahwebbishere) and facebook.com/sarahwebbwriter.

Mollie Cinnamon is stuck on the snoresville island of **Little Bird** with her great-granny while her TV-presenter mum films a new show. Mollie is bored, bored, **bored** until she makes friends at the **Songbird Cafe.** Disaster strikes, though, when the cafe is threatened with closure. Can Mollie and her new friends save the cafe?

Little Bird Island has been Sunny's home ever since she was **adopted** from China. **Sunny** loves to spend time baking and drawing at the **Songbird Cafe** – if only her anxiety didn't stop her from speaking to her friends. Could a trip to **China** be the key to unlocking Sunny's **voice**?